DEMONS AFTER DARK
COVENANT

INFERNAL GAMES

WRITTEN BY

JENNA WOLFHART

Infernal Games

Book Two of Demons After Dark: Covenant

Copyright © 2021 by Jenna Wolfhart

Cover Art by Fenix Cover Designs

All rights reserved.

❀ Created with Vellum

1

My boss was the opposite of a demon. And because of that, I hated him. As the clock ticked over to five, Mr. Winchester bustled out of his office door to give me a watery smile. His brown suit was wrinkled in the front, though his shiny shoes were polished to perfection. He never wore them on the sidewalks, always changing out of tennis shoes when he got to work.

"It's five now. Thanks for doing a wonderful job, Luna. You may go now." His eyes lingered far too long on my V-neck blouse, and then he vanished back into his office. Even though he stayed until well past eight most nights, he always sent me home the second my shift was over. I knew I should be thrilled. Ever since Az had found me a job and an apartment with my new fake name, my life had never been easier.

1

And yet, I'd never felt more anxious. It was like my skin wanted to jump off my bones and run.

Not from New York. Not from my past, like I'd done the past several years of my life. Everything within me wanted to run straight to *Infernal*.

With a heavy sigh, I powered down the computer, pushed up from the desk, and grabbed my bag. Time to head home and have another night just like the one before. And the one before that. Ad infinitum.

I'd plop down on the tiny sofa inside my Brooklyn walkup, feed my pigeon, and watch *Friends* reruns until my eyelids fell shut. I'd seen that damn pivot episode too many times to count. And still laughed every time.

As crazy as my month with Az had been, it had definitely never been dull.

Not that it matters, I thought as I rode the elevator down to the ground floor. My weeks with Az hadn't been boring, but they *had* been dangerous. I'd nearly been killed. And so had Serena.

Staying away from Asmodeus was the best thing I could do.

Not to mention that damn contract he'd made me sign. The rules were clear. If I put a single toe inside *Infernal* ever again, I'd lose my soul. What that meant exactly? I still wasn't sure. But it clearly wouldn't be pleasant.

The elevator doors whirred open. I trailed through the lobby and stepped out onto the bustling Midtown streets. For a while, I let myself get lost in the city's energy. I had nowhere to be and no one to see. My best friend, Serena, had been swamped at work for the past several weeks. Every other friend I'd made during my time in New York City worked at that damn club I couldn't go near.

I blew out a frustrated breath as the summer breeze rustled the red strands around my face.

I wanted to *do* something. Life stretched out before me, full of limitless possibilities. No one knew who I was anymore. Mia McNally didn't exist. Well, she did, just... not here. I was Luna Adams, a hopeful transplant who'd moved here from the south to make it in New York City, just like thousands of other girls my age. I didn't want to go back to my empty apartment. Not yet.

So I wandered through Times Square and smiled at the tourists posing beneath the blazing lights. I dodged taxis charging by and ducked around a guy with a guitar who wore nothing more than an American flag as underwear. I wandered down Fifth Avenue, glancing at the designer bags that cost more than my entire life savings, which was... not much. Even with a job, I barely made enough to pay for rent and food.

But it was enough. I didn't need designer bags or fancy shoes.

In fact, I didn't need anything or anyone but myself, my best friend, Serena, and my favorite pigeon in all of New York.

My heart lurched as my mind instantly popped another name into my thoughts.

And I need Az.

I gritted my teeth and forced that thought away, following the streets downtown. Obviously, I didn't *need* Az. Logically, I knew I was better off without him in my life. He was an asshole most of the time, and he'd brought me nothing but trouble. Also, he was, you know, an actual demon from the underworld. Sure, we'd had a moment. But he'd made it clear that night had meant nothing to him at all.

It had only been sex. It wasn't like it had meant anything to me, either.

I certainly *never* wanted it to happen again.

So why had I just walked myself all the way down to Hell's Kitchen?

I sighed, folded my arms, and leaned against a light pole. Just across the street, *Infernal* sat closed and dark. Even after hours spent wandering through the city, it was only seven o'clock, and the club wouldn't open for a few more hours. It was one of those late-night places, a fancy, glittering watering hole for wealthy supernaturals.

Instinctively, my hand curled around my necklace. I'd kept his signet ring all this time and wore it day and night, just in case. Rumor had it Lucifer was in Manhattan. And he wanted to find me.

Obviously, *that* couldn't happen. So if he sought me out, I needed the ring's blasty thing to use against him.

4

Of course... standing right outside Az's club probably wasn't the best way to avoid Lucifer. It was just...dammit, I was curious, okay? The literal King of Hell had come to New York, and I was dying to see what he was like. Did he have horns? Gleaming red eyes? Did fire pour off his skin?

If you looked at him wrong, would he smite you?

Plus, I couldn't get Serena's words out of my mind. Lucifer didn't *just* want to find me. He wanted me to become his bride.

My biggest question was: *why?!*

A few times, I'd picked up my phone to call Az and ask him about this whole thing. What exactly did Lucifer want with me? And if he found me, would he take me back to Hell with him? Put a ring on my finger and carry me across a threshold of flames?

I shivered just thinking about it.

With a deep breath, I pushed away from the light pole and minced across the street. The club might be shut, but I knew the Legion was likely inside. They seemed to hang out there at all hours of the day, doing...Legiony stuff. There were a few small windows in the back alley next to the rear door. Maybe I could just take a small peek inside, see if I could get my eye on Lucifer, and then high-tail it out of there.

My blood burned in my veins as I whispered around the back corner of the building. This was really a terrible idea. I wouldn't lie to myself and pretend it wasn't. I'm smart enough to know when I'm doing something dumb. But I just flat-out didn't care. If I sat still any longer, I might have to do something drastic. Like snoop on a Legion of demons, apparently.

Besides, a little peek into a window wasn't breaking the rules, right? The deal only said I couldn't step foot inside the club. As long as my feet stayed firmly outside, no big deal.

I just had to make sure no one saw me. Lucifer especially.

With a deep breath, I clung to the shadows, tiptoeing down the alley. I'd spent enough time at *Infernal* to know there were a few windows along the back edge of the building that looked into the club. Unfortunately, it looked like I'd have to stand on top of a dumpster to get a glimpse of anything going on inside.

I folded my arms as I stared up at the green monstrosity. A sticky yellow substance oozed from the cracks, and the scent of rotting fish swirled around me. I wrinkled my nose. Gross. I'd have to clamber on top of that thing and get that gunk all over my clothes and hands—at the very least. This blouse was one of the few I had that was suitable for work, and I needed a few more paychecks before I could buy any more. Was I really this desperate to find out what they were up to in there?

Honestly, what the hell was I doing? This was beyond idiotic. I needed to leave. Now.

Pulling the humid Manhattan air into my lungs, I took a step back. I laughed and shook my head at myself. *Honestly, Mia, this is one of the dumbest things you've ever done.* And to think I'd almost gone through with it.

Thankfully, I'd seen the light. By way of dumpster goo. I twisted on my heels, turning toward the opening of the alley, just as a deep, melodic voice drifted into my ears.

"I've done everything you've asked of me. How much longer do you plan on staying? Your presence in Manhattan is making everyone nervous."

Chills swept down my arms as my entire body clenched tight. I knew that voice. I'd recognize it anywhere. Deep, rich. The first time I'd heard it, he'd reminded me of melted dark chocolate.

A shudder went through me in spite of it all. I still hadn't forgiven him for so easily pushing me away, but I couldn't help the way my body felt drawn toward that voice.

Asmodeus continued. "The fae especially. They've stopped coming to the club. You know how long it took for them to feel comfortable around the Legion when I first opened this place."

"And one might wonder why the fae ever decided they were comfortable around you. Could it be because you've changed sides?" The voice was even deeper and darker than Asmodeus's. With it came a sharp blast of unease that sent tremors down my spine. I shuddered, turning my eyes up to the open window. It was as if darkness itself lived inside that voice. And there was no doubt in my mind who it belonged to.

Lucifer.

I should run—get out of there as fast as I could. If he found me spying, there was no telling what he would do.

My feet stayed glued to the pavement. I held my breath and waited for their next words. I couldn't help it. My curiosity was beyond my control at this point.

"I thought we were past that," Az replied in a dark tone that suggested he was only seconds away from biting off Lucifer's head. Surprising he would speak to his King that way, but it wasn't like I understood how Hell worked.

"Eisheth's testimony goes far, but Rafael does not lie. You know this, Az."

"And he was mistaken. Rafael has had it out for me for years, and he read into things he didn't understand. We've gone over this, Lucifer. I am fully on the side of Hell."

Lucifer sniffed. "Yes, well, that still doesn't explain what happened to Mia McNally."

A low growl rumbled from within the club. "She escaped. She ran. If I could find her, I would. Her soul is mine."

Shivers stormed across my skin at the sound of

my name on Lucifer's lips, as well as Az's response. I knew he was only saying that to hide the truth from the King of Hell, but the danger in his voice was as hot and electric as evil itself. It sounded like he wanted to rip me limb from limb. If I were Lucifer, I'd be convinced.

But I knew better than anyone just how good Az was at pretending.

They must have drifted away from the window because their voices dropped to nothing more than a murmur. I craned my head, trying to make out their words, but I didn't have enhanced supernatural hearing like they did. *Dammit.* They were talking about me, and I was desperate to know what else they said. It might mean the difference between surviving another year in Manhattan or... marrying the devil himself.

Yep, so I was definitely going to climb on top of the dumpster now. I edged closer to it and latched my hands around the top, grimacing when my skin made contact with the goo. I tried not to think about what it might be and hauled myself over the top of the dumpster.

My muscles groaned, and the metal shuddered beneath my weight. Wincing, I slowly pushed up into a crouch and peered inside the club.

My breath caught in my throat when I spotted Asmodeus. It had only been a few weeks since I'd seen him, but it felt like far longer than that. Years, maybe. Centuries. Or maybe I was just being melo-dramatic.

Tall, muscled, and brimming with power, Asmodeus was unlike any man I'd ever known. Probably because he wasn't a man at all. Demonic energy pulsed from his skin in silken strands of shadows. As I'd gotten to know him, I understood what the presence of his shadows meant. He was either very happy or very, very angry. Most likely the latter. Not a good look if he wanted to convince Lucifer I meant nothing to him.

Speaking of Lucifer...my eyes drifted to the other figure in the dark club. My mouth went dry. He was wider and more muscular than Az, and elaborate tattoos swirled across the back of his neck and down the length of his left arm. He wore his silver hair down past his ears, and golden rings glimmered on strong, powerful hands.

Hands that were clenching. His head jerked to the side, and slowly, he turned toward the window that I hovered beside.

I let out a yelp and ducked down. The metal wobbled beneath me, knocking me off balance. My boots skidded across the yellow slime and sent me tumbling off the dumpster.

Arms windmilling, I landed in a heap on the alley pavement. My knees buckled; my hands flew out to brace my fall. All my breath shot out of my throat as a storm of bright spots blinded me momentarily.

I shook my head and blinked away the shock. Lucifer had *definitely* heard me creeping around on the dumpster. And if he'd heard that, there was no chance in hell he'd missed my shriek and tumble.

Time to run.

2

I threw myself to my feet and charged down the length of the alley. Blood seeped through my jeans where my knees had slammed into the ground, but fear powered me. I just kept running, despite the flashes of pain.

The mouth of the alley loomed large before me. Sucking in a deep breath, I threw myself out of it and swung a left, away from the entrance to *Infernal*.

My heart pounded in my ears as I considered my options. I could keep running until I reached the nearest entrance to the subway, where I would promptly take a train to Brooklyn. Apparently, Lucifer didn't like crossing the East River, whatever that was all about.

Of course, he had wings. If he were following me, he'd no doubt take to the skies and search for a red-headed idiot flailing her way through the downtown Manhattan streets. He'd find me before I reached the subway.

Or I could hide and hope he hadn't spotted me yet.

I slowed to a stop and tipped back my head to gaze at the smog-infested sky. No sign of those massive, powerful black feather wings that Az and the rest of his Legion sported. I assumed Lucifer had a pair, too. So that was good, at least, right?

But it probably wouldn't stay that way for long. I whirled on the spot, searching for a hiding place that the King of Hell wouldn't think to look. My eyes landed on an old cathedral, whose spires scraped the low-hanging clouds, on the corner of the block.

I smiled and raced down the rest of the street, ducking inside with my heart pounding out a rhythm against my ribs. Thankfully, the place was open, even if it was almost eight o'clock by now. I pushed away from the door and peered inside. A lofted space stretched out before me, broken up by rows of wooden pews. They all faced a small stage draped in red velvet carpet. A cross hung on the wall behind it, and candlelit sconces flickered with flames. The place was empty other than that. The silence pounded against my eardrums.

Shivering, I hugged my arms to my chest and hovered by the door. As eerie as it was, at least I would be safe in here. The question was, how long would I have to wait before I could leave? Would I have to camp in here all night?

A heavy thunder sounded from behind me. I whirled on my feet, heart skipping like a rock on water. Asmodeus stood before me, inky ribbons of shadows swirling across his skin. Danger flickered in his ice-blue eyes like flames from Hell. He growled and strode toward me, his hands fisting by his sides.

I sucked in a breath. My heart nearly stilled. "Az."

He growled, his eyes narrowing. "What the hell do you think you're doing?"

"Um." I wet my lips and cast a glance behind me. "Thought it might be a good time to pray?"

His eyes darkened even more, if that were even possible. "You were at *Infernal* tonight, poking your head in where it doesn't belong."

"Oh, that."

"Mia." He grabbed my shoulders and gave me a gentle shake. "What the hell were you thinking? Your soul is on the line. We made a deal."

"We did. And it said I couldn't step foot inside your club." I gave him a wincing smile. "But the deal said nothing about me peeking through the windows."

God, that sounded way weirder when I spoke it out loud.

He let out a heavy sigh and closed his eyes, as if he were on the verge of losing his patience with me. My heart flickered, and a strange sorrow whorled through my gut. I'd imagined our reunion over and over in the weeks since we'd said goodbye, and it was never like this—tense, uneasy, layered in anger and disappointment. I'd pictured him sweeping me up in his arms and carrying me back to his penthouse, where he would spoil me with gin and tonics and pancakes.

Not this.

"Lucifer heard you." His words felt like punches to my gut.

I grimaced. "Yeah, I thought that might be the case. Hence the church. I figured he might not be a fan of this place, so he wouldn't think to look here. Also, I thought demons might not be allowed inside." I eyed him warily. "But I guess demons are more welcome here than I realized. Did you see me run inside?"

His lips flattened. "No, I followed your scent."

"Oh." A fresh wave of unease rushed through my gut. If Az had my scent, then...

"Lucifer caught it, too, and he knows it's yours." He tightened his grip on my shoulders. "We have to get you out of here now. He won't be far behind me."

"That's not ideal," I said as lightly as I could. When I'd made the ridiculously hasty decision to spy on them, I hadn't known this whole scent thing could be an issue. "How long will he remember my scent? A few hours?" I paused. "Don't tell me it'll be days."

He closed his eyes. "Until Lucifer leaves Manhattan and stops looking for you. It's been weeks since I saw you, Mia, and I still know your scent. It would take years for me to ever forget it. And his senses are far stronger than mine. Now that he knows you, you're forever imprinted in his mind."

My stomach bottomed out. "Right. That's great."

"Come on." Az wrapped his arm around my shoulder and steered me out the door. A sudden sharp *zing* went through my gut, a sensation I hadn't felt since the last time I'd seen him. It brought a strange sense of *deja vu* along with it, reminding me of something I couldn't quite grasp.

Did he feel it, too?

I started to ask him, but then stopped when he rushed me into the quiet streets. Dread pounded against my skull as we darted through the shadows lining the buildings. I swallowed hard as my boots splashed into grimy puddles from the recent summer rain, fighting the urge to glance behind me. Had Lucifer seen us? Was he just behind the next corner?

What would he do to Az if his King caught him trying to save me?

Fisting my hands, I let out a yelp of surprise when Az dragged me into the alley behind his club. I stumbled back when he released his grip on my shoulders, shaking my head. "Why are we here? Isn't this the last place we should be?"

He pointed at the dumpster. "Get inside."

My mouth dropped open. *"What?!"*

"Get inside the dumpster, Mia. Now." The heaviness in his voice told me he wasn't joking.

"You can't be serious." I took a step away from him. "I'm not climbing into a New York City dumpster. There *must* be a better place I can hide." One that didn't reek of rotting fish and cat vomit.

He growled and stalked toward me. "If you don't climb inside that dumpster, then I'll throw you in there myself."

"Um." I wet my lips, my eyes darting around the alley for an escape hatch. "I think I prefer my church option, personally."

He threw up his hands and darted toward me faster than the blink of an eye. With a grunt, he hauled me into his arms and leapt up on top of the dumpster, where we landed with a metallic thump. Before I could throw myself out of his arms, he'd yanked open the left side of the dumpster.

The world yawned wide. Darkness swallowed me as I tumbled toward the piles of trash. I landed in a heap, arms and legs akimbo. My face pressed against a particularly gelatinous takeout bag.

Anger churned in my veins as laughter drifted

down toward me. Asmodeus hovered at the edge of the opening, peering down at me with that stupid dimpled smile of his. "This is the best I've ever seen you."

"Fuck off."

"Come on." He knelt and held out a hand toward me. "We got the scent off you now. Time to go before Lucifer gets back."

"I ought to pull you in here with me," I spat back as I grabbed his hand.

He arched a brow. "You're welcome to try."

Growling, I gave a little tug. But he was like a massive boulder. Impossible to budge. It didn't even look like he had to make an effort to stop himself from falling in. Ugh. So freaking annoying.

Az yanked hard and pulled me back into his arms. The takeout bag was still stuck to my skin like a limp jellyfish clinging on for dear life. And then the world fell out from beneath me once more as my fake demon ex-boyfriend took to the skies.

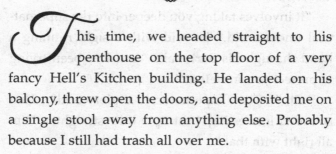

This time, we headed straight to his penthouse on the top floor of a very fancy Hell's Kitchen building. He landed on his balcony, threw open the doors, and deposited me on a single stool away from anything else. Probably because I still had trash all over me.

"Can I take a shower now?" I asked through

gritted teeth, still angry he'd thrown me in with the goo I'd tried so hard to avoid.

"Absolutely not. We need to keep your scent hidden for as long as possible." Frowning, he paced the length of his penthouse. "And we need to find a way to make you invisible to Lucifer. Permanently."

"Okay, great. And how are we going to do that?"

He stopped pacing and turned toward me. "There are methods. Ones I'd rather not use."

Lovely. I shivered.

"If they're bad enough a demon finds them unpalatable, then maybe we should brainstorm a little more." I gave him a weak smile. Truth was, despite my bravado, I was seriously regretting my idiotic decision to spy on some demons. Not only did Lucifer have my scent now, but I'd ruined any chance of a movie-esque reunion with the sexiest man I'd ever laid eyes on.

I stank. And I probably had goo on my face. Not my most shining moment, and he had to witness it all.

Of course, he'd also been the one to cause my current condition.

"It involves taking you deeper into the supernatural underworld," he said with a sigh, running a hand through his dark hair. "And I've been trying to protect you from that."

"Oh." The supernatural underworld? That sounded interesting. I sat up a little straighter. "I'm all right with that."

He gave me a dark look. "Did you forget how close you came to dying on multiple occasions the last time you got involved with supernaturals? You're mortal. This life is far too dangerous for you. Honestly, Mia, why did you have to come back to *Infernal* tonight?"

I pressed my lips together, more to hold back the truth than anything else.

Because I've missed you.

But I couldn't say that. Not when he looked at me like...this. Like I was a pesky child who'd stumbled in during an important client meeting. He couldn't wait to hand me back to the nanny.

"Serena told me Lucifer was in town, and I couldn't resist." I shrugged. "No one is telling me anything. I wanted to see just how much he knew and how long he planned to stick around."

"Well, he was close to leaving." Az folded his arms, leaning back on his heels. "After tonight, it'll be weeks more before he gives up. We need to change your scent and get you out of Manhattan."

My hands fisted. "Not this again. You can't force me to leave my home."

"It's the only way." He strode toward me and took my shoulders in his powerful hands, gently this time. His eyes darkened as he peered down at me, like he was peeling back layer after layer of my soul. Not for the first time, it felt as though he could see into the very depths of me. My deepest, darkest

21

thoughts. My greatest fears. And the desire I felt for him still, even after everything.

"I swore an oath to keep you safe," he murmured, edging so close that I could smell the flames of Hell wafting from his skin. "And I never break my oaths. You can't stay here anymore. You have to leave tonight."

3

"What in the actual hell is going on now?" Serena bustled into Az's glittering penthouse wearing a pristine pantsuit in shades of glorious blues, the bright color popping against her dark skin. Her hair cascaded around her shoulders in perfect waves, and the light makeup she'd applied highlighted the deep color of her eyes.

She looked like an absolute *boss*.

One that was not happy to see me.

She glared and dropped her briefcase by the door. "Mia, please tell me that Az's text was some kind of joke and that you didn't decide to snoop on the actual King of Hell tonight."

I grimaced. "Well…"

Her eyes practically rolled back into her head as she sighed. "Mia, why? I thought we all made it clear you couldn't go near the place. What about the deal you signed?" She shot Az a panicked glance. "Is she going to lose her soul? Did she break the deal?"

"No," he said around his clenched jaw. "She took a tumble while she was spying. She could have very well fallen through the window. But thankfully, she only slid off the top of the dumpster and landed on the pavement."

Serena wrinkled her nose as she drew closer, her eyes flicking across my stained blouse. "Clearly."

"Oh, don't let him fool you." I shot Az a glare. "I look—and smell—like this because *he* tossed me into the dumpster."

Arching her brow, she turned back to Az. "You did this to her? Don't make me get out my claws."

"It was to get rid of her scent."

"Ah." She nodded, relaxing. "Good going."

"We need to find a more permanent method," he said as he gave her a meaningful look. For a moment, all they did was stand there staring at each other while a weird, tensed silence peppered the air. Every now and then, one of them flicked their eyes my way. For a good, oh, ninety seconds, before I'd had enough of it. With a frustrated sigh, I pushed up from the stool and stepped between them.

"I don't like this. It's like you two are having a silent conversation."

Serena lifted her shoulders in a small shrug. "We are. Kind of. He's trying to make a suggestion to me, and demons can be *very* suggestive."

My stomach did a little flip. "Suggestive?"

"It's one of their powers. The Princes are especially good at it. However..." She smirked at him. "It doesn't work on everyone."

"Hold up." I whirled on Az and jabbed a finger into his chest. I winced when my skin met unyielding rock. Ouch. "Are you telling me you can convince people to do things just by looking at them?"

"No. I can *suggest* things." He smiled, though his dimples didn't make an appearance. They hadn't all night other than during the dumpster incident. Typical. "That's much different than convincing someone to do something."

"It can be pretty convincing," Serena muttered. "But not to me, or most supernaturals. It works best on humans."

"Please tell me you've never done that to me— convince me to do something with your demon magic." I couldn't help but ask, thinking back to the many times I'd felt drawn to him. When he'd pressed me against the wall. When I'd climbed on top of him, on the very dining table that sat just behind us. I flushed, horror twisting in my gut. Had all that happened because he'd messed with my mind? Surely not...

Az pressed his lips together as his expression went dark. "You still don't trust me. After all this time."

A pang went through my heart at the betrayal in

his eyes. Az, I'd learned, could not stand it when anyone questioned his integrity. He'd been burned in the past, just like I had. Only what had happened to him had been far worse. A woman he'd trusted had destroyed one of the demons in his Legion. And the Legion was his family.

"You just tried it on my best friend," I pointed out.

"No," he said evenly. "I made a *suggestion* to her. Nothing more than that. The truth is, we are in a terrible position. Lucifer wants you, and he doesn't believe the story I've tried selling him. He especially won't believe it after tonight. And when he finds you, he will take you to Hell and force you to become his bride. Serena told you, didn't she? What he wants with you?"

I winced. "Yeah, she might have mentioned the bride part. But what I don't get is why?"

"I don't know." He shook his head. "He won't say."

"Doesn't that strike you as a little odd?" I said, edging off the stool to take a step toward him. "I mean, I'm just a random human he's never even met. What would be the point? Surely he doesn't just go around taking human brides all the time."

Or did he? Was that his thing? Pretty weird if so.

"Not typically, no." Az strode toward the floor-to-ceiling glass door that opened out onto his balcony. My eyes caught the tension in his back and the way his suit jacket stretched tightly across his

26

broad shoulders. Something was bothering him. Something more than what he said. It seemed like there was always another secret to uncover with him.

"Well, then why? It doesn't make any sense," I tried, casting a quick glance at Serena. She merely shrugged. Her life might be firmly entwined with the supernatural world, but she knew as much about Lucifer as I did at this point.

"Unfortunately, I don't think we can worry about the whys right now." His hands fisted by his sides, his back still facing me as he stared out at the twinkling city lights. "None of that matters more than getting you to safety. We need to mask your scent and get you out of New York before he can find you."

"No," I said, taking a step back. "I told you before. I'm not leaving New York."

It was my home. The only one I had left. Sure, my only friends were supernaturals who I couldn't see or contact for fear of being found by the literal King of Hell. And sure, I was going by a fake name and hiding out in an empty apartment most of the time. New York was loud and hard and often reeked of a million different disgusting things. But it was still the only place in the world I wanted to be.

When I walked down the streets, I could feel the pulse of the city beneath my boots. This place was alive, and it made me feel that way, too.

Plus...it had Az.

"Mia," Serena whispered from beside me. I twisted toward her to find unshed tears bubbling in her eyes. "Lucifer has caught your scent. He won't give up until he finds you. Staying in New York will mean..."

"Hell," I whispered back, my gut twisting.

She nodded. "If you don't leave, you'll be ripped away from here anyway. Lucifer will not stop until he finds you."

I let out a shuddering breath. This day really had not gone according to plan. Maybe it had been a bad idea not to choose *Friends* reruns over spying on a demon club.

"You know why I asked you here, don't you?" Az asked quietly, finally turning to face us. His frame was back-lit by the city lights, drowning his face in shadows.

Serena nodded. "I have a pretty good idea. And I'm not convinced it's the right move."

"She'll be safer that way," he replied, avoiding my gaze. "Hidden. Stronger. If he ever figures out what we've done, she'll have the means to protect herself."

I narrowed my eyes. "Um, could we possibly not talk in riddles please? What exactly are you suggesting we do?"

Serena took my shoulders in her hands and squeezed tight. Her eyes searched mine with an intensity that sent shivers down my spine. I'd been on edge before, but something about the way she looked at me shook my soul. Whatever Az had come up with, I wasn't going to like it. It was probably dangerous. And it would leave me reeling for weeks.

Anything he did had a tendency of doing that.

"The only way to mask your scent is to change you in some fundamental way," she said in a harsh whisper. "As long as you are *you*, Mia, anything we do is temporary. This disgusting dumpster smell will fade quickly even if you don't shower."

My heart flipped over. "So I have to jump into a dumpster every day. Maybe live in one? That's what this is all about, right? Nothing more than that...right?"

Not that I liked the sound of living in a dumpster. Talk about hitting rock bottom.

She pressed her lips together and flicked her gaze toward Az. With a heavy sigh, he trailed over to us and placed a firm hand on my shoulder. For comfort and solidarity, no doubt. But his touch had the opposite effect on me.

That eerie, familiar *zing* shot through me, singeing my core and making my ears ring. I sucked in a sharp breath, tensing. His eyes met mine, flames flickering deep within the ice blue shards. Those flames bored into my soul, filling me, consuming me, until I wasn't entirely sure where I ended and the fire began.

"Ahem," Serena said.

My cheeks flushed, and I ripped my gaze away from Az. What was it about him that caused that kind of reaction in me? Was it because he was a demon? No, it couldn't be. As fond as I was of the Legion, being around them never made me feel like this. Like I was unmoored.

"Your blood needs to change," Serena said in a rush of words, cutting through my thoughts. "It's the only way to permanently change your scent. That means turning you into something else. It means saying goodbye to your humanity, Mia."

"What?" I whipped my head toward her, certain I would see laughter in her eyes. But her face was as cold and stony as the steel buildings of Midtown. Her lips were flat, and her eyes were hard. She meant every word. My heart pounded my ribs. "You can't be serious."

Az tightened his grip on my shoulder. "Trust me. This is the last thing I want to do. If there was another way, I'd choose it in a heartbeat."

"There *is* another way," Serena said. "The fae. But there's no guarantee they'd say yes, and they'd probably ask for something in return."

"And we might not get to them in time. I don't want to risk taking Mia back out on the streets until her scent is fully gone."

"Plus, Lucifer might suspect that's what you'd do." Serena frowned. "He'd probably never guess you'd be willing to hand her over to a vampire or a werewolf."

I tried to take a step back, but Az held me firmly in place. "So that's what this is all about," I whispered, wildly casting my eyes from one face to the next. "You want to make me a werewolf."

Those were absolutely the most bizarre words I'd ever spoken aloud, and I'd said some crazy shit over the past couple months. My best friend and my former fake boyfriend wanted to turn me into a furry, full-mooned beast.

"Yeah, kind of," Serena whispered. "Sorry, Mia. The best way to mask your human scent is to turn you into something else. Something that could not only hide you but help you protect yourself."

Something else. I would be...a supernatural.

With a strange prickling sensation rushing across my skin, I lifted my eyes to meet Az's intense stare. "All right."

He frowned. "You're agreeing to this?"

"What did you expect me to do?" I whispered, fisting my hands by my sides. "Let Lucifer hunt me down and kill me? No thanks. A werewolf sounds like the better option to me."

"I thought you'd run screaming out the door."

A wan smile lifted the corners of my lips. "I don't run screaming, Az. I thought you'd figured that out by now." And then I turned to Serena, who was regarding me with an expression I couldn't quite read. "So what now?"

"I have a strange feeling," she whispered, her dark eyes widening. "Something's off."

Az jerked his head her way. "What do you mean something's off?"

She shook her head, stepped in close, and then dragged a sharp, painted nail across the width of my shoulder. I winced as pain lanced through my arm. Blood bubbled up in the wake of her mark, bright red and angry.

I held my breath and waited for something to happen. Was that...it? Would I transform right now? Would they be able to control my beast form and stop me from hurting anyone? For the first time since Serena had suggested this crazy plan, a lump of unease rolled through my gut. We hadn't prepared for this. What would happen if I turned into a beast right here and now?

They'd need to chain me. I'd seen Serena when she'd first turned all those years ago. She'd been out of control.

Serena huffed out a breath. Az's jaw clenched tight.

"What's happening?" I asked, half-hoping they'd refused to answer. They both looked like a baseball bat had smacked them in the face. "Have I sprouted fur or something?"

"No," Az growled. "It's worse than that. You're immune."

4

"Immune?" I frowned, certain I hadn't heard him right. "How the hell could I be immune?"

Az folded his arms. "You tell me. Immunity to werewolf venom does not happen accidentally."

My brows rocketed up to my hairline. "You think I did this on purpose?"

"How else could it have happened?"

"Ugh!" I shot back, snapping my head toward Serena. "Tell him he's being ridiculous. I couldn't have found immunity to werewolf venom when I didn't even know it existed until now!"

But Serena's frown merely deepened. "He's right though, Mia. If you're immune, there's a reason. No human alive can withstand werewolf venom."

"Apparently, at least one of us can."

"Something must have happened," Az said as

33

he paced the length of his penthouse. "Perhaps someone gave you immunity when you were younger, and you didn't realize. Did anyone else in your town know that Serena was a werewolf? Your parents, perhaps?"

I snorted. "My parents never had a clue. And if they'd known, they would have forced me to stay away from Serena. I can't imagine they would have been open-minded about me having a werewolf for a best friend."

"Someone else then," he muttered. "What about your parents, Serena? Did they know? Who turned you?"

Serena shrugged. "They never knew, either, and I can't remember who turned me. I know what night it happened, but everything else is a big shadowy blur. Mia's the only one who knew the truth about what I am before I came to New York."

He stopped short, halfway between us and the kitchen. "Well, someone must have known, and he —or she—sneaked Mia an immunity serum. That's the only explanation for this."

I nodded, frowning. Az seemed so sure about what had happened, but it didn't sit right in my gut. Who would have done that? When would it have happened? I thought back to my childhood and everyone in it, trying to find a point where it might have happened. But...there weren't any answers to those questions. I'd never had a great memory when it came to my childhood, and that certainly wasn't improving now. Like Serena had said, it was all just a blur.

So maybe Az was right, and I just didn't remember. Someone could have found out and tried to protect me from Serena's werewolf side. It wasn't the craziest idea I'd ever heard.

It just...it didn't feel *right*.

"So what now?" I asked quietly, flicking my eyes to the yawning windows that looked out on Manhattan. Lucifer would think to look here soon, even if he couldn't follow my garbage-drowned scent. All he'd have to do was shoot up above the buildings and see me standing here in the brilliant light of Az's penthouse. I was a sitting duck.

"We'll have to find another way to mask your scent," Serena said with a sigh, slumping against the wall as if her legs could no longer stand to hold up her weight. "There *are* other ways. A vampire could work. Werewolf immunity and vampire immunity are two entirely different things."

"Absolutely not," Az said with a dangerous growl. "Werewolves hold on to their humanity. Vampires don't. She'd become someone else. A bloodthirsty, vengeance-fuelled monster. A murderer."

My heart twisted in my chest. "So that's out then."

"And then there's the fae," Serena added. "You could ask them for a scent glamor."

Az's scowl deepened. "There's a reason I didn't

go to them in the first place. If they even agreed to it, they'd ask for something in return. The fae give nothing away for free, and their deals are..."

"Worse than yours?" I arched a brow. "If I remember correctly—and I do—I'm pretty sure I signed a deal with you, *unknowingly*, for my soul."

"That was..." he began.

"Different?" I folded my arms. "I don't think it's any different at all."

He ran his fingers through his thick, dark locks. "You don't know what they'll ask for. If you did, you might not be so eager to seek them out."

"Is there another way?" I asked him.

Slowly, he closed his eyes and let out a heavy sigh. "I could carry you away from here and hide you in a tomb where Lucifer could never find you."

"I'm not going to spend the rest of my life in a tomb, Az."

"I had a feeling you were going to say that," he muttered.

I stepped up to him and slowly wrapped my hands around his. His eyes flipped open, and the flame-edged blue pierced the very depths of my soul. Breath hitching, I kept my gaze firm and unyielding. But I couldn't help but soften at the torment in his eyes. It was hard to stay angry at him when he looked at me like this.

Like he would tear the clouds from the sky if it meant he could keep me safe.

"I need to do this, Az. It's the only way."

"Fine," he said. "But if a fae even looks at you *slightly* wrong, I'll rip off all their heads."

"*W*e need to be quick." Az pressed his lips against my ear, tickling my skin. My hair whirled around me in a tornado of red as the city rushed by beneath us. I tried to calm my racing heart, but it was next to impossible. We were flying. Far above Manhattan. My feet dangled beneath me like lead weights. If Az let go of me, I would tumble to a very terrible death. Roadkill on pavement.

I clutched his neck and buried my face in his chest. Maybe if I didn't see the ground far below us, I could forget exactly where we were and what we were doing. "Fine."

"Your scent is growing stronger," he murmured. "It won't be long before Lucifer catches it again."

"Please don't toss me into another dumpster," I muttered.

Although…that might be a better option than what we were doing now. At least then I would have contact with the ground.

Az rushed us through the skies, aiming his sights on the Lower East Side. At least we didn't have to go far. He landed in a back alley, away from the glow of the nighttime city lights. A red-brick building sat just behind us, rising four stories high.

Dilapidated fire escape platforms creaked in the light summer breeze.

"Now what?" I whispered as he slowly unwound his arms from my waist. I wet my lips as I stared at his hands, wishing I could draw them back to me.

No. I mentally kicked myself. I couldn't get carried away. He'd made it more than clear that what we'd had was nothing more than a one-night stand fuelled by a little acting that we'd both gotten *way* too carried away with. That and gin. Lots of gin.

Besides, I didn't want to go there again. It had been fun, but he was a demon who was very unavailable. I refused to let the tension between us get into my head—and somewhere else, a little further south on my body.

I cleared my throat, stepping back.

"Now we wait." He turned toward the dilapidated building and stared expectantly at the wall.

"The fae live there?" I arched a brow. "Not sure why, but I expected something more like Central Park."

He grunted. "That would be too obvious. The fae are devious, Mia. Never forget that."

"Like demons aren't?" I said with a smile. "I've met Phenex remember. Not to mention Caim."

A low growl rumbled from his throat, and I bit back a satisfied smile. There it was. The uncontrollable jealousy he felt toward me and Caim. Not that he had any reason to be jealous. I liked Caim. He'd been nothing but welcoming and kind, but there was no spark there. Not like I felt with Az.

And yet he couldn't *stand* the idea that I got along with anyone else.

Still. Even now.

My thoughts were interrupted when the grungy wall shimmered before us. The red bricks warped and wobbled as if I was looking at a pool of water instead of a building. Flowers sprouted and vines shot up toward the sky. I blinked, and it was all gone. The building had been replaced by a grove of trees, hidden just behind a wrought-iron gate covered in roses.

I sucked in a breath, awed and overwhelmed by the clear magic of this place. I'd learned a lot about the supernatural world in the past couple months, but I'd seen nothing like this.

"So that's a thing that just happened," I whispered.

I could hear the smile in Az's voice when he replied. "The fae like to show off."

"I don't blame them."

"The building is an illusion. Some of this might be, too. Remember that. Everything you're about to see cannot be trusted. You never know what's real and what's fake when it comes to the fae."

I turned to glance up at him. "Can you do anything like this?"

His face hardened. "No. If I could, we wouldn't

39

JENNA WOLFHART

be here right now. Come. Take my hand. Don't let go of it."

I slid my fingers into his warm hand and smiled as he tugged me through the arched gate. The scent of sweet blossoms filled my head, and a strange dizzy lightness swirled through my limbs. A lopsided smile spread across my face, and all the tension I'd felt before vanished like mist. Suddenly, I couldn't remember why we were in such a terrible hurry.

"This is nice," I said happily, squeezing his hand. "We should do this more often."

He cut his sharp gaze my way. "That didn't take very long."

I cocked my head. "What didn't?"

"Their magic. It's effecting you already." He frowned, and I couldn't help but laugh at the confusion on his face. Big, brave, terrible demon. He looked so confused. It was cute. "That normally doesn't happen."

"I guess I'm a big ol' weirdo," I said with a shrug. "Immune to werewolves, but not to fae!"

He shot me a curious glance as we drifted further into the fae's strange woodland escape amidst all the stone and steel. And then he took a sniff. A *sniff*. Asmodeus actually sniffed me. "Impossible."

I cocked my head. "What's impossible?"

"Nothing," he muttered, tightening his grip on

40

my hand. "You're one of the most human humans I've ever met. You couldn't be anything else."

My jaw dropped as I followed him through a particularly prickly bush. How much further would we have to walk through these woods? "You're not saying you think I'm a...what? Werewolf?"

He shook his head and tugged me close as a tall, curvy woman stepped out from behind a vine-drenched door. Her long curly hair hung to her waist, coils of tightly wound pink. A silky blue dress hugged her frame and matched the sparkling color of her eyes. She gave me a once-over and then frowned at Az.

"Az, you know I have nothing against you personally, but I thought we told you we don't like demons here. The fae get antsy." Her voice was husky and deep, and the sound of it sent a new storm of shivers across my skin.

"The fae are always antsy," he replied, his tone warmer than I'd expected, especially after the way she'd spoken to him.

She grinned. "Don't I know it? Even so, you know how things are. Lucifer's in town, and everyone is on edge."

"This won't take long," he said quietly, turning to me. "This is Mia."

Her eyes widened. "Ah, Mia. The one he wants."

"Unfortunately."

"And you brought her here?" She leaned forward and gave a little sniff. "You've covered her

41

in garbage, which means you've come here for a favor. You want to hide her with a scent glamor. I should have known. The rumors are true. You're in love with this girl."

I sucked in a sharp breath. Heart hammering, I glanced up at Az. But his outline wavered like a desert at the hottest time of day. That damn magic. It was making it difficult to think. And apparently, it made me imagine things.

Because this fae clearly couldn't have said that Asmodeus, the Prince of Hell, was falling in love with me.

He could barely stand me most of the time.

Right?

"You know the problem with rumors, don't you, River?" he asked in a dangerous voice. "They get twisted and torn. Shred into a million pieces until there's nothing left but a hint of the truth."

"So you don't love her."

"I'm just trying to keep her safe. She wouldn't make it in Hell."

Tears burned my eyes as I twisted away. There was no reason to get upset by what he'd said. Of course he didn't love me. I was just a pesky human he'd pretended to date. It had been nothing more than that. And yet...my stomach still churned. My heart ached. His words had been so dismissive of me.

She wouldn't make it in Hell.

"I think you'd be surprised." River folded her arms and lifted her brows. "You can't tell, can you?"

Az's hand tightened around mine.

"Tell what?" he demanded.

"I can't do a scent glamor on her because she already has one."

Sweat beaded on my brow, and that *zing* went through me again. The one I'd only ever felt when Az looked at me. But it was happening now as this fae sized me up like a steak on a platter. Dread roiled through me.

"What do you mean?" I whispered.

"Interesting," she murmured. "*You* don't know, either."

"I've had enough," Az muttered, yanking me to his chest and wrapping his arms protectively around me. His heart thumped against my ear, fast-paced and frantic. I didn't know what to think about that. That he was as nervous as I was.

"She's not human, Asmodeus," River called as he dragged me toward the gate. "Something has been done to her to hide who she is, and she doesn't even know it's happened." She levelled her gaze with me. "If I were you, I'd want to find out what she is."

5

"**T**his can't be happening." Az paced, brow furrowed.

River lowered me into a wooden chair at the edge of the trees. Whispers drifted out from the dense brush, and I swore I saw the flicker of several yellow eyes. None of the other fae ventured out to join us. It seemed River was right. They didn't want to greet the demon.

"Mia is human." He came to a sudden stop before me and peered into my eyes. *Zing.* "She looks like one, she smells like one, she *feels* like one."

River shrugged. "Whoever did this to her is strong—someone as strong as me. It's impenetrable magic, invisible even to demons."

Az narrowed his eyes. "How many fae are as strong as you?"

"Not many," she said lightly, brushing my hair

45

JENNA WOLFHART

back from my shoulders. She gave me a kind smile, but I didn't miss the eager excitement in her eyes. River might be helping us, but she was getting something out of this. What? I didn't know. But I needed to stay on guard. "In this area of the world, maybe ten."

He strode over to us, looming tall, shadows whorling across his skin. "Can you tell who did it?"

"Maybe if I had more time." She glanced up at him. "But I'm assuming you'd like this done quickly. The garbage smell has faded. Unless Lucifer has stopped actively tracking her, he might already have a lock on her location."

"Do it," he said, shoving his fingers into his midnight hair. "Go on then. Get it over with."

"You know I can't do this for free," she said lightly.

"Just do it!" He shouted. His voice echoed through the trees.

Smiling, River brushed her fingers along my collarbone, lighting up my skin with the same kind of magic that had melted my brain as soon as I'd stepped into the grove. My body burned like it was engulfed in flames. Wincing, I glanced down at my arms, half-expecting to see the fire I felt. But there was nothing there. Nothing but—

A strange scent wafted into my nose. A familiar scent, but one I couldn't place. It was harsh and metallic, almost like gold. *Ozone.* The word popped into my head, though I couldn't explain where it had come from. What did ozone smell like exactly?

It smelled like this.

Az sucked in a sharp breath and stumbled away from me. River's hand fell from my arm, and her wide eyes whipped across me in disbelief. She pressed her fingers to her lips. Dread clenched my heart.

"What's going on?" I whispered.

Az's jaw tightened. Hell, his whole body did. He shot a sharp glance at River, who still stared at me like she'd seen a ghost. "Are you sure she doesn't know?"

"It seems impossible, but yes." River let out a shuddering breath, leaned forward, and peered into my eyes. "She's been carefully hidden."

The words sent a boulder tumbling through my belly. My voice wobbled when I finally found the words. "You two are freaking me out. What's going on and what the hell is that *smell*?"

Az shook his head, and I could practically feel the hectic thumping of his heart, though that had to be impossible. I couldn't *hear* his heart beating. Right?

But suddenly, I no longer knew what was impossible or not.

"Mia, I need you to stay calm," he said in a low voice that did little to actually calm me. "What I'm about to tell you is going to be a bit of a shock."

"I'm a supernatural," I said flatly, pushing up

from the chair. "You've confirmed it. But how? Why? When? Did a werewolf get to me when I didn't know it? Is that even possible? Wouldn't I have shifted at some point? I—"

"You're a fallen angel." He gently grabbed my arms when I stumbled back, as if someone had punched me in the gut. Mind reeling, all I could do was gape at him. I couldn't have heard him right.

"No," I said, shaking my head. "That's impossible."

He pressed his lips together. The steadiness of his gaze was the only thing that kept me from screaming and running in the other direction. Desperation rose within me like a hurricane. I wanted to get away from this. I didn't want to hear any more of it.

My entire life flashed in my mind's eye. A childhood spent running barefoot in the grass. Dancing on stage. Sitting at a desk doodling in math class. It was all there. My very human life. *I am not a fallen angel.*

"Someone has gone to a lot of trouble to mask the truth of you," he murmured, still holding me steady. "I can't begin to explain it, but it's the only possibility. Someone found you when you were born and made sure you would never know what you are."

A shudder went through me. "But why? None of this makes any sense, Az."

"I don't know." He ground his teeth and pulled

back, casting a glance at River. "Unfortunately, we can't waste any more time talking about it right now. We need to mask your scent."

"What?" Brow furrowed, I glanced between them. "Why? If this is what I smell like now, won't that stop Lucifer from knowing who I am? You wanted to change me. Well, I'm pretty sure I'm changed."

Understatement of the century.

River stepped closer and pushed my hair behind my shoulder. A kind smile softened the tension on her face. "Lucifer knows every angel and demon in this world. While he won't recognize you as Mia McNally anymore, he will wonder at the sudden appearance of a new fallen angel in Manhattan. It's not worth the risk. Not until you find out more about your past."

I sucked in a sharp breath and stepped back. "You think Lucifer is the one who's done this to me. You think he knows I'm...whatever this is."

"Maybe," Az said softly. "It might explain his determination to find you."

Dread coiled around my heart. My mouth went dry. "I really, really hope you're somehow wrong about all this."

He took my hand in his and squeezed tight. Warmth travelled up the length of my arm and settled around my heart, soothing my frayed nerves. Just a little. "I know, Mia. Me too."

"You ready?" River placed her hand on my

shoulder and smiled. "How about we give you a werewolf scent glamor? You feel comfortable with that? Or...I could always make you smell like fae, if you'd prefer..."

"No," I said, clearing my throat and dragging my gaze away from Az's piercing eyes. "A werewolf is good. I've known Serena all my life. That feels...right."

Although, if I were being brutally honest, nothing about this felt *right*. It felt like the ground itself had been ripped out beneath my feet, and all I could do was swim in the open air and hope I didn't plummet into the boiling core of the earth. There was no time for my mind to wrap itself around this new development. No silence to think.

Because if I stopped now, Lucifer would find me.

River squeezed my shoulder, and that strange fiery heat blazed across my skin. Moments later, she stepped back and cocked her head with a smile. The scent of ozone whispered away. "There you go. You're all good to go."

And now we owed her one.

After we said goodbye, Az led me back into the streets. The hidden grove of trees melted from view as soon as our feet hit the grimy alley pavement. The old, dilapidated building shuddered back into place, hiding the fae's secret home from prying human eyes. Az's entire body was tense, his surging emotions matching mine. I could tell by the way the shadows roared across his skin.

Silently, we strode out of the mouth of the alley and hightailed it across the bustling street. I didn't know where he was leading me now, and I didn't care. I was a fallen angel. One hidden for years. How could that even be possible? How could that be *me*?

It seemed insane. Maybe all of this was a mistake.

"Az." I grabbed his arm and stopped him before he kept rushing through Manhattan as if nothing strange had happened. "We need to talk about this."

"I need to get you out of here first." He towered over me, his muscular body rippling beneath his fitted suit. "If Lucifer was the one who did this, I can't risk him getting anywhere near you, even with your new scent. There will be a reason you've been hidden. And it won't be a good one. I can guarantee you that."

Chills swept along my bare arms. "And it's why he wants to marry me."

His gaze went dark. "Most likely."

"I don't want to leave." Lifting my chin, I fisted my hands by my sides. "I want to stay and figure out what the hell is going on. None of this makes any sense. I have no powers. I don't even have heightened smell or anything. I grew up in Tennessee with human parents and a human sister. I was born in a small town outside of Nashville.

There are photos of me. If I'm a fallen angel, how could any of that be true?"

Az gave a hard shake of his head. "He'll have done something. I don't know what. But something. And he's one of the few beings powerful enough in this world to have done it."

"So let's—"

"Hello, Asmodeus." A dark voice slithered into my ears. My heart lurched into my throat, and my entire body went hot. An eerie, unsettling sensation raced down my spine. Sucking in a breath, I slowly spun on my feet to face the demon who had joined us on the sidewalk.

All I saw was death.

Dark, piercing eyes. Tense, cutting jawline. Vengeance and anger swirled around him like a storm cloud—invisible, but it packed a punch all the same. Or maybe I was just imagining things.

"Lucifer," Az said slowly, drifting toward his King so that his body blocked mine like a shield. "What are you doing here?"

A lazy smile lifted the corners of Lucifer's full lips. "I might ask you the same thing. You rarely leave Hell's Kitchen, particularly for a street like this. No fancy restaurants. No lounges. No luxury shops. I know how much you like shiny things and your little toys you play with."

"I was taking a walk." Az's words were short and packed a punch.

Lucifer's eyes drifted to me. "With?"

I cleared my throat. "Sansa."

Shit. The name popped out before I could stop it, and I really wished I could turn back time and take it back. Why, oh why, did I give him the name of a freaking *Game of Thrones* character? Surely he would see through that.

Did Lucifer know about *Game of Thrones*?

He chuckled. "Nice to meet you, Sansa." Then he sniffed. I tried to hold back my cringe. These demons and their weird sniffing thing. "Tell me. Have you ever been to *Infernal*?"

Az stiffened.

"Um." I wet my lips, unsure of how to respond. Probably best to be as honest as possible so the lies were easier to track. "Once or twice."

"Good." He nodded. "We have an opening there for a dancer. You have a nice figure and beautiful red hair. Quite unique, your look. I'd like you to come work for us."

My brow shot to the top of my forehead. *What the fuck?!* "That's...a great offer. But don't you want to see me dance first?"

His smile stretched wide. "Sure. Why not? Come dance at the club for one night. If you're terrible, you're fired. Otherwise, you can stay as long as you'd like. How does that sound?"

"Erm, well, I don't know. I—"

"Sansa," he purred, stepping closer. Az stayed firmly between the two of us, but it felt like it hardly mattered. If Lucifer wanted to get to me, he could. I

53

had no doubt about that. "You know who I am, don't you? Every supernatural does. Don't pretend you don't all whisper about me behind my back."

I swallowed hard. "Lucifer. The King of Hell."

"That's right." A wicked smile curled his lips. "And no one says no to me, especially not a little wolf. You will come dance at *Infernal*. Tonight. If you're good, the job is yours. And I will not take no for an answer."

Well, shit. So much for Az's plan to keep me as far away from Lucifer as possible. Of course, maybe this wasn't such a bad thing. I'd been dying to step foot inside the club. I'd have a chance to find out more about what was going on. And...

Wincing, I glanced up at Az. I'd forgotten one very important thing. I couldn't step foot in *Infernal*. Not without losing my soul. And I couldn't say no to Lucifer, either. I had a feeling he'd make his displeasure very, very clear if I did. By ripping my spine from my body? Or tossing me into the Hudson River? That didn't sound appealing, but neither did losing my soul.

I'd have to convince Az to destroy the contract. It was the only way.

I gave Lucifer a tense smile. "I guess I'm in."

6

When I stepped one leather black boot inside *Infernal*, I expected something terrible to happen. Like for the heavens to open up and smite me right then and there. My soul was bound to this place. I'd made a deal with a demon to stay the hell out. But when I walked through that black door, nothing happened.

Interesting. Did I even have a soul? If I really was a fallen angel—and I still wasn't one hundred percent convinced that I was—did that mean a demon contract even meant anything?

Maybe I was immune, like I was to the werewolf venom.

"Ah. Here we are." Lucifer smiled and led me down the hallway toward the dancers' dressing room. My heart pounded as we drew closer. The girls would have no idea what had happened in the past few hours. When they saw me, would they greet me the way they always had? I cast an uneasy glance up at Az, who silently strode on my other side, but he avoided my gaze. Shouldn't he do something? This could all come tumbling down on us in less than a second.

Lucifer pushed open the door and dragged me inside. The chattering suddenly hushed, and half a dozen eyes peered at us from beneath thick lashes and carefully curled hair. He pressed a hand to my back, and I fought the urge to wince away from him.

"This is Sansa," he announced to the room. "Your new dancer."

Priyanka slowly stood from her stool beside the bank of mirrors, wrapping a colorful silk gown around her hourglass frame. Her face was entirely unreadable. "Hi, Sansa. Welcome to the crazy house. Come on in. We'll help you get ready."

Her voice was even and unbothered. Good. I doubted if I spoke, I'd sound that relaxed. Lucifer frowned but drifted out the door with Az, leaving me alone with the dancers. A heavy breath whooshed out of me, though my nerves felt like they'd been shot with a bolt of high-voltage electricity.

Priyanka gripped my elbow and dragged me over to the mirrors. She sat me down and then pulled her stool over close. Her raven hair curtained her face as she dropped her voice to a whisper.

"Why are you here? What the hell is going on? And why, dare I ask, do you smell like a werewolf? Don't tell me you've been turned."

I arched a brow. "You can tell?"

"Honey, we can *all* tell."

"You all have enhanced smell?"

"Of course we do." She glanced behind her at the girls gathering around us. "We're supernaturals."

Strange, since apparently I was supposed to be one, too. I couldn't smell a damn thing other than their perfume and hairspray.

Quickly, I filled them in on what little I knew. They shifted uneasily on their feet as I told my story. There were a few shocked gasps. Hands lifted to lips. And Priyanka's grip on my knee tightened so much I could feel her sharp nails through my jeans.

"Holy shit, Mia." Priyanka's eyes flicked across my body. "A fallen angel? Really? What does Az think about this?"

"He seems confused." I pressed my lips together. "We haven't had a chance to discuss it beyond that. Lucifer swooped in and dragged me back here right after we left the fae."

She leaned forward and sniffed. "Well, River did a hell of a job, and it's a good thing Az took you to her instead of to me. Lucifer's been lurking around here all day. He would have caught us. Even if he suspects something, he won't be able to prove it. Nothing about you says fallen angel to me."

"Right. Because I should have powers. And I don't."

Her brow furrowed. "It is strange. You've never had enhanced hearing? Or extremely good eyesight?"

I shook my head, my heart tumbling through my chest. This was why I couldn't get past this bizarre development. In the movies, the secret supernatural always has some kind of power, hints that there's more to them than meets the eye. But I literally had nothing. I was just a girl lusting after a demon and trying desperately to stay alive.

"Well, we'll have to figure it out later." Priyanka let out a sigh, shook her head, and stood. "I'm sorry. I know you want answers, but we can't get them right now. We have to dance. Lucifer has been...difficult to deal with since he arrived in Manhattan. If we don't do what he expects, he makes life very difficult for us."

I blew out a breath and took her offered hand. "I don't like this. The whole thing is strange. Why would he have asked a random werewolf he met on the streets to come dance here?"

She arched her brow with a meaningful look in her eyes. "I think you know."

My heart pounded. "Even with the scent glamor, he suspects I'm me."

With a pat on my shoulder, she nodded. "Probably."

My mind spun with possibilities. This was really bad. I needed to get out of here. If I went out there now, I might never get to leave.

"So what if this whole thing is a trap to get me in that cage? What if all he's doing is setting me up? He could lock me in there and never let me out. Not until he takes me to Hell."

"We've got your back," she said firmly, glancing behind her at the girls, who nodded in agreement.

"Against the King of Hell?" I asked in a small voice.

As much as I wanted to believe them, surely they couldn't go against him without risking everything. *Infernal* was a front. The Legion was only pretending to be loyal to Hell. In secret, the demons and everyone else who worked for Az tried to save human souls. Lucifer could *never* find out. If he did, he'd drag Az and his Legion back to the underworld.

"We've got your back, Mia," Priyanka repeated in a determined voice. "You're one of us. You have been since that first night you walked through the door. And we will always protect our own, no matter what."

Tears blurred my vision, and her words filled me with twisted hope. These people felt more like a family to me than my own ever had. It didn't matter that I'd been gone for several weeks. They'd welcomed me back with open arms, zero questions asked.

Okay, so there'd been a few questions. But only to make sure I was okay.

"Can I ask you something?" I said when Priyanka turned me toward the mirror and plucked a mascara wand from the table. The other girls gave me encouraging pats on the shoulder and drifted back toward their own mirrors. We had no more time to waste on chitchat. The club doors had opened, and the patrons would expect us to take to the stage within the half hour. *Lucifer* would expect us to dance. And I had a feeling that whatever Lucifer expected, Lucifer got.

She leaned in, angling the wand toward my eyes. "You can always ask me anything."

"What brought you to *Infernal*? Did you know what the Legion was doing before you agreed to work here?"

I'd only arrived via a flyer taped to a random light pole in Brooklyn. Was that how Az typically recruited new members to his inner circle? Or was there more to it than that? He was so guarded, so untrusting. I couldn't imagine him hiring someone straight off the street.

Of course, that was *exactly* what he'd done with me.

A soft smile flickered across Priyanka's face. "I imagine it was pretty similar to how you got hired. I saw an ad for a dance opening and dropped in for an audition. He turned me away at first, but then came knocking on my door a few days later. That's when he told me what he was and gave me the whole spiel about saving souls. From that moment on, I was in."

I transformed into a marble statue as she flicked my lashes with the wand. "So he turned you down at first, just like me."

"Yep," she said. "Talking to the other girls, he did the same with them. We think he likes to look into people before bringing them into the circle. He needs to see what kind of person they are. Decide if they can be trusted. What he's doing here, Mia, it's important. He's not only saving souls, but his work could mean the difference to whether or not the world ends."

A shudder went through me. This whole thing went far deeper than what was happening to me. This was a game for the future of this world. A deadly game. One that could end in eternal flames.

All those weeks ago, Az had placed his trust in me, hoping my presence by his side would help him stop the King of Hell from winning. And here we were again after my curiosity had come so close to ripping everything apart. I had to do my best now to convince Lucifer I was exactly who I said I was, and no one else.

Because if he found out Az really was hiding Mia McNally, he'd have the confirmation he needed. He'd know Az had turned against him. I couldn't let that happen.

After Priyanka finished my makeup, I changed into a sexy slip dress hanging from the clothes rack in the back corner. The girls kept the changing room stocked with new outfits designed to catch eyes. The shimmering silver reflected the overhead lights, the material hitting my mid-thigh. The plunging neckline clung to my breasts, making it look like I actually had some cleavage.

We walked out from backstage and climbed into the cages to the roar of the crowd. The patrons of *Infernal* loved the dancers and treated us like stars of a Broadway show. The gilded cage shuddered beneath my feet as it lurched toward the ceiling on a heavy metal chain.

My belly did a little flip. I'd done this over a dozen times now, and I still got as nervous as I had on day one. There was something about being locked in a cage far above ground that made my nerves skitter like spilled candy on a marble floor.

Not shocking, really. I was *trapped in an elevated birdcage*. If I *didn't* get nervous, I'd be a little concerned about my mental state.

The music pumped through the club. Pulling a deep breath into my lungs, I danced. It was easy to let go of my anxiety when the notes swirled through my head. I closed my eyes and focused on the beat, letting my body take over and giving my mind a rest.

But then I felt him and his gaze on me. As I swayed inside the cage, I popped my eyes open to find Lucifer lounging against the wall in the back corner of the club. His arms were folded over his chest, and he stared straight up at where I danced.

Terror squeezed my heart.

I swallowed hard and tried to glance away, but I felt locked in place. I couldn't move. I couldn't look anywhere but at his face. A shudder went down my spine. There was a darkness in his eyes I could see from even here. And anger.

There was no doubt in my mind he knew exactly who I was.

I tried not to panic. Priyanka had promised they wouldn't let anything happen to me. But honestly, how could she stop him? Lucifer was the strongest, most powerful supernatural in this room. He could burn us all to ash if he wanted.

I would not put the odds in our favor.

My eyes slid across to room to find Asmodeus. He stood in the opposite corner. Unlike Lucifer, not a single inch of him was relaxed. His entire body practically hummed with pent-up power. Hands fisted by his sides, he glared across the club at Lucifer, who hadn't seemed to notice his First Prince was looking at him like he wanted to rip off his head.

As if he sensed me, Az glanced up. Our gazes locked, and that old familiar *zing* went through me again. That weird thing was happening more often these days. In any other situation, I might spend some time wondering why, but I was too distracted by the tense stand-off between two of the most powerful demons in the world.

Because of me.

Suddenly, I could read his thoughts as if they were my own. The reason Az looked like he wanted to rip Lucifer's head off was because…he was actually considering doing it. My blood curdled in my veins.

He wouldn't. Would he? And what would happen if he did?

Lucifer would destroy him.

Suddenly, I felt Lucifer's attention shift. With a sharp gasp, I turned back toward him, my body still moving to the beat. To anyone else watching, they'd have no idea a storm was brewing in this club. I'd gotten good at putting on a show during my weeks spent as Az's fake girlfriend. I knew how to pretend.

Lucifer's eyes tightened on Az. The two demons stared at each across the crowded club, and my heart rocketed up into my throat. Shadows rippled across Az's face, darkening his expression.

Distracted, I tripped on my own feet. I stumbled to the side and hurtled toward the cage bars. My head slammed into the steel. Blood pounded between my eyes from the blinding pain. I let out a cry and fell to my knees, holding my hands to my head. When I pulled my fingers away, they were covered in blood.

The music cut off. The crowd hushed. Az ripped open the cage door, gathered me into his arms, and then flew—on his beautiful, massive black wings—out of the club.

7

Az carried me into the Legion's meeting room and deposited me into a folding chair. The others trailed inside. Caim was first with his blinding smile—though it wasn't so blinding now. Concern rippled across his handsome features instead. Valac followed. His bleached white hair fell into his hooded eyes, and Phenex charged in beside him. Bael and Stolas edged into the door, casting each other uneasy glances.

"You all right, Mia?" Caim knelt in front of me and peered into my eyes. His familiar face blurred before me.

"My head feels like it was beaten with a hammer," I muttered.

Ouch. Even talking hurt.

"Did Lucifer see?" Valac asked in that unnerving, unearthly voice of his. I felt something ripple along the back of my neck as he turned his piercing gaze on me, like he was peeling back all the layers of my skin. I shuddered.

"Valac," Bael warned in his lilting British accent. "Mate. How many times do we have to tell you not to do that to Mia?"

"Sorry," Valac muttered.

"Lucifer saw," Az said, angling his body in front of me. "We need to heal her quickly before he gets back here."

I blearily peered up at him. By this point, he was nothing but a bundle of dark shadows. "Why does it matter? Werewolves can bleed."

I knew from experience. I'd watched Serena patch up her wounds after a full moon night spent racing in the woods. I never asked too many questions when she came back like that, but she always had at least one monstrous gash on her legs.

"They heal quicker than humans," he said, kneeling before me. "A little cut like this would take hardly any time to heal."

I pressed my shaking hands to my forehead. "It doesn't feel like a little cut."

"Trust me, it's smaller than a seed."

"And I'm not human," I whispered.

The Legion didn't shout cries of alarm or demand for me to explain myself. That could only mean one thing. Az had already found a chance to tell them. Not surprising. The Legion was his family. These demons were his brothers, not by blood but by choice. That made it all the more binding. He told them everything. And I do mean everything.

A relief, really. I didn't want to have to explain tonight's bizarre revelations to anyone else. Especially when I didn't understand any of it myself.

"True," he said darkly. "But it's clear that you don't have access to any supernatural powers. That means I'm going to have to take care of the problem for you."

"You can do that?" I asked, even though deep down I already knew the answer to that question. He'd never said it outright, but Az had healed me more than once. I'd just never been conscious for it until now.

The thought of him pouring his magic into me brought on a little tickle between my thighs.

Dammit. Now was definitely *not* the time for those kinds of thoughts.

I just couldn't help myself. Not when it came to Az.

"He's coming," Stolas barked from the door. "Hurry up, Az."

Az palmed my knees. His feverish hands skimmed across my skin, making me forget about everything and everyone else. Suddenly, we were alone in this room, and all the pain and worry and fear melted beneath his touch. I stared into the flickering depths of his eyes and saw something I'd never seen before.

Recognition. A reminder of the past. But how?

I'd grown up in Nashville, Tennessee, and had never been to New York until I'd moved here four months ago. The chances we'd ever met before were slim to zero. I leaned closer with my breath caught in my throat. His tongue whispered across his bottom lip.

Desire curled through me.

He blinked and pulled back. "You're healed."

His voice was gruff and distant and hard. All the emotions I'd seen in his eyes were gone, as if he'd pulled a shutter across them. Frowning, I glared up at him. Not this again.

"Why do you always have to—"

"Everything okay in here?" Lucifer breezed into the room, the Legion parting like the Red Sea. Power pulsed on his bronze skin as he came to stand before me. He cocked his head. "You hit your head pretty hard out there. Is the wound not healing?"

His fingers touched my forehead. I stiffened and sucked in too large a breath. The gasp practically echoed in the silent, tense room.

"Hmm." His hand dropped away. "It's hot to the touch but feels fine. Looks like your werewolf healing powers kicked in just in time. Why is everyone gathered in here as though that little cut was an emergency? An overreaction, is it not?"

"Sorry," I muttered. "I guess I'm just a wuss when it comes to blood."

Probably not the best response, but it was too

late to take it back now. I didn't know much about werewolves in general, but I knew a hell of a lot about Serena. And she didn't hate blood. In fact, in her wolf form, she craved it.

"You're a very odd wolf." He sniffed, and then shot me a wicked smile. "Best get back to dancing. I heard several of the regulars talking about you. They like the way you move."

My head jerked toward Az. *That* probably wasn't good. Some of the regulars would know me from before. *Shit, shit, shit.*

He gave me an almost imperceptible nod. The look in his eyes was clear. I needed to follow orders. Better do whatever Lucifer said.

Shakily, I stood and took the towel Caim offered. I wiped the blood from my hands and squared my shoulders. Time to get back to dancing then. No time to waste. Be a puppet on a string for Lucifer's amusement. Just as I reached the door, Az grabbed my hand. Something rough slid between my fingers. His eyes caught mine, heavy with meaning.

I gave him a smile and drifted out the door, my heart pounding. He'd slid me a note.

"Asmodeus, you truly do have a strange relationship with some of your employees," Lucifer said, his voice fading as I strode down the corridor. None of the others followed me. I was on my own now. They'd already done too much. If they hovered, like I knew they wanted to, the roots of

Lucifer's suspicions would only grow deeper. And we'd already planted enough seeds.

With a steady nod to myself, I tucked the note into the corner of my bra.

The night went by quickly. I tried not to think and instead just let the music move my body the way it wanted. The lights blurred before me as I swirled, and the cheers from the crowd fed me like a massive plate of fluffy pancakes.

I didn't know what would happen when this night was over, but right now, I didn't have to think.

All I did was move.

When my shift was over, I ducked into the ladies' room before the girls could pepper me with a million questions about my accident. I sucked in several deep breaths and pressed my back to the door. There was something I needed to see before I did anything else. Hands shaking, I unfolded the note Az had passed me.

My eyes tripped across his words, hastily scrawled in deep black ink.

Meet me on the Brooklyn Bridge at four.

My heart hammered my ribs. Unfortunately, Az didn't mean four in the afternoon. Limbs heavy, body aching, all I wanted was to crawl into bed and sleep my stress away. But I couldn't. Deep down in my bones, I knew the night was far from over.

I was a supernatural. Maybe. And Lucifer had dragged me back into *Infernal*.

Could I even return to my apartment in

Brooklyn now? It was full of my stuff. My very human stuff that had no hint of my supposed were-wolf identity. The whole place probably reeked of my humanity. If Lucifer followed me back there, he'd know in an instant who I was.

Pain flickered in my heart.

Even after everything I'd done and as hard as I'd fought, I was homeless. *Again*.

My hand fisted around the note as my gaze dropped to the grimy floor of the club bathroom. I was back in my worst nightmare all over again. The one I'd thought I'd left behind for good. Homeless. Jobless. Friendless.

Only I wasn't, I reminded myself. The Legion, and everyone who worked for *Infernal*, had surrounded me in solidarity. And while I couldn't go back to my receptionist job now, I truly didn't care. I'd been bored out of my mind. So while I didn't have a home or an actual job, I had friends.

I just had to trust Az to take care of the rest.

With a determined nod to myself, I flushed the note and turned toward the mirror. I winced as my eyes scanned my face. I'd looked better, that was for sure. My eyes sported some purple bags, and my red hair was wilder than a cluster of thorny bushes. Unfortunately, there wasn't much I could do to fix that right now.

When I tiptoed out of the bathroom, I hung a left toward the back door that led right into the alley that had started this whole thing in the first place.

As I stepped outside, I pulled the cool night air into my lungs and tried to relax. No such luck. I hadn't seen Lucifer on my way out, but that didn't mean he wasn't watching me...and following closely behind.

Despite our sneaky little attempt at covering up who I really was, I knew we'd done a piss-poor job of it. He'd know about the hidden fae court and why we'd go there. I wasn't an idiot. Lucifer probably knew way more about Manhattan than anyone else did. He'd been around for...how long exactly? Since the beginning of time? It boggled the mind.

Some of the *Infernal* regulars had already seen me dance. They might not have known my name when I last worked at the club, but they'd known I was involved with Az. We'd been flagrant about it. If Lucifer had heard them talking...

Shaking my head, I picked up my pace, casting an uneasy glance over my shoulder after every fifth step I took. No sign of him yet. Or any other supernatural serial killer. The fallen angels, Rafael and Michael, were probably back from Hell. Would they pick up where they'd left off?

For the first time in my life, I wished I could hide my blazing hair. It made me far too conspicuous.

Shockingly, I actually made it to the Brooklyn Bridge without incident, but fear kept pumping through my veins like acid. One of the things I loved about New York was the energy that pulsed through the streets, no matter the time of day or night. But it was four o'clock, the small pocket of time between the night owls and the early birds. The partiers who stayed out late had drifted to home by now, but dawn was still an hour away. No runners plodded down the bridge, and commuters were still in their beds.

It was so quiet. Too quiet.

I wet my lips as the wood groaned beneath my feet. The bridge rose before me, the beams reaching out like eager fingers toward the sky. In the distance, I spotted Az's unmistakable form. He hovered toward the center of the bridge, arms braced on the railing. As I strode toward him, my heart flipped. Strength pulsed from his body. I could feel it rippling in the wind, travelling to me on invisible wings.

Strength, and...violence.

Sometimes, it was easy for me to forget that he was a demon, but I'd seen the raw power of him the night of the Covenant Ball. Just before the sacrifice, he'd stalked toward me, feral vengeance in his eyes. The mask he wore for the world had fallen away to reveal the truth. He was *extremely* dangerous. And he would do *anything* to protect his Legion. Guilt-free.

That included ripping an enemy's head off his— or her—body.

"Mia," he said, as I approached him. His stubbled jaw clenched as he kept his gaze forward, focused on the rippling East River far below us.

"Az." I joined him on the edge of the bridge, popping up to sit on the wooden railing beside where he stood. "What's with the cloak and dagger routine?"

"You know."

I sighed. "Yeah. Though I'm not sure why you wanted me to meet you on the Brooklyn Bridge. It's not exactly private."

"Lucifer hates the East River. He won't come out here."

I arched a brow. "You mentioned that before. Why?"

"No one knows."

"It seems there's a lot about Lucifer no one knows."

"Just how he likes it." Az nodded. "His fear of the East River is one of the reasons why we chose Manhattan as our home base. The river is always here if we need it, though only in emergency situations. Avoiding him only raises his suspicions."

I sighed and leaned against one of the bridge's beams. The cool metal bit my skin. "Seems like his suspicions are already sky high. Why did he want me to work at the club? Why do I smell like a fallen angel? Have I lost my soul because I went into *Infernal*? What's going on, Az?"

Tears blurred my vision, and I blinked them away. As close as I was to totally losing it, I had to keep my shit together. Breaking down was not an option. I had to stay strong.

"For once, I know nothing more than you do." He gripped the bridge with his powerful, tense hands, leaning out over the edge to gaze down at the rushing river. "As for the contract...I ripped it up the day after you signed it, knowing you'd end up breaking our deal eventually. Couldn't risk you losing your soul. I just didn't know it would be so soon."

On any other day, I might have laughed or grumbled at him for being so sneaky. I should have known. He'd secretly ripped up our last contract, too. Az would never truly risk me losing my soul. He might be a demon, but he was not the monster the world thought he was.

"What are we going to do, Az?" I whispered.

He seemed to sense my fear, or maybe he just heard it in my voice. Releasing his grip on the railing, he palmed my knees. Every cell in my body lit up like flames. His warm hands soothed me, even as they transformed my stomach into knots. The flecks of ice in his eyes softened as he leaned in close. The scent of him curled around me, driving away the fishy scent of the river. We were the only ones on the bridge, and his fingers were dangerously high on my thighs.

It almost made me forget why we were here.

"There's only one way to end this. If it were up to me, I'd send you as far away from Lucifer as I could." His words snapped me back to reality. I opened my mouth to argue, but he continued before I had a chance. "But that won't work. He caught us near River's home, and he suspects we've hidden the truth about who you are. If I take you away from here, it will only confirm his suspicions. We're going to have to play along with his little game, Mia."

All the blood rushed out of my face and pooled in my gut, heavy and thick like lead. I'd had a hunch we'd have to go this route, but hearing it out loud made it all too real.

"If he really thinks I'm...well, *me*, then why hasn't he just taken me straight to Hell already? Why dance around it like this?"

His dark gaze swept across me. Tension rocketed between us. "This is Lucifer, Mia. *Everything* is a game to him. And if we want to win, we're going to have to play."

8

V alac peered at us with bleary eyes, his front door swinging open. He wore a wrinkled black t-shirt and loosely fitting sweatpants. Just past his muscular frame, a yawning penthouse glistened beneath the pink sunrise streaming in through a bay of massive windows. Turned out Valac had a penthouse, too, only two blocks south of Az's building. Damn, these demons were rich.

"I'm going to need Mia to stay here for a while," Az said by way of greeting. "Her apartment is off-limits now."

Valac rubbed his eyes. It was odd seeing him like this, so odd it almost made him seem normal. *Almost.*

"If that's what you need, then of course. But is there a reason she can't stay with you?"

"Lucifer knows Mia and I were...involved. He'll

expect her to stay with me. If she doesn't, it throws him off his game."

Shrugging, Valac stepped aside and motioned us through the doorway. "Very well. Come on inside, Mia."

Frowning, I trailed into the apartment, Az following close behind. His logic made sense in a very demonic game kind of way. But I still had questions.

"I've got to be honest. I don't see how this is any better. Couldn't he still find me here?"

"Sure." The whites of Valac's eyes bored through me. "But I already have a couple of roommates. Dancers from the club. It makes more sense for you to stay here than at Az's place. There's a precedent in place. This doesn't give Lucifer any ammunition."

"Sure. All right." I closed my eyes, weariness tugging at my bones. "This is ridiculous. You know that, right? It sounds he's just going to bide his time and wait for us to take one wrong step."

"Yes," Valac replied, his voice harsh and full of darkness. The sound reminded me that, of all the demons, he unnerved me the most. The others, while strong and powerful and edged in danger, could almost come across as human at times. Not Valac. There was something so otherworldly about him. The haunted look in his eyes told me he'd seen things that had shattered his soul.

And now I had to live with him.

"What about Hendrix?" I asked, twisting to Az. "He'll be all alone in my apartment."

His lips twitched. "Already taken care of."

I let out a sigh of relief. "Good. Poor thing. I hate that I keep shuttling him around New York every few weeks."

"He doesn't mind," Az murmured, his eyes flicking across my face. "As long as he's with you."

Something inside me squeezed tight. An overwhelming urge churned my gut. All I wanted was to drape my arms around his neck, press my face against his chest, and feel him surround me, blocking out everything else. The past twenty-four hours had been a whirlwind, and frankly, I felt fried to a crisp. I didn't want to stay here. I wanted Az's apartment. His bed. His arms. All of him.

Nothing against Valac, of course. He was kind to let me stay with him. But let's be honest, he wasn't Asmodeus, the First Prince of Hell.

Az's fingers twitched by his sides, and for a moment, I thought he felt that same impossible tug between us. And then we'd forget about tricking Lucifer and give in to this connection while we still could. He'd collect me in his arms and take me home. Damn the consequences.

"I should go," he said in a hoarse voice, ripping his gaze away from mine. "You've had a long day, and you should get some sleep. We'll have an assignation in the morning."

Assignation. I couldn't help but smile fondly at

that. Just another one of his little word quirks that gave him away as someone far older than what he looked. An immortal demon. One, I had to finally admit, I had feelings for. Dammit.

We said our goodbyes, and Valac led me into the living room. His place was sparser than Az's, giving it an echoey, vacant feel. There was a single stone-grey sofa facing the windows. A tiny round table sat just beside it, holding a stack of well-worn books. My boots clicked against a floor that looked a lot like stone.

I hugged my arms around my chest as I gazed down a skinny hallway. Several shut doors lined the wall.

Valac saw me looking. "Bedrooms. The girls are both asleep. Long night at the club."

His eerie voice echoed through the looming space. He turned his gaze on me, and for a moment, fear rattled my heart. It felt like he wanted to peel back the layers of my skin. He would burrow into me and shatter my bones. After a moment, he shook his head and glanced away.

"Sorry. I know you don't like that."

My heart tumbled. "What even is it? You've done it before."

"I'm reading you," he murmured in that eerie voice. "Would you like me to show you to your room?"

My room. If only. I didn't have a room. Anywhere. For the past couple of years, I'd drifted through life without roots, going from one place to the next, never staying anywhere long enough for my heart to grow fond of it. It was starting to wear me down.

I sighed and closed my eyes. Memories of the night flashed through my mind like a horror film reel. And the worst part about it was, this was all my fault. If I'd kept my stupid curiosity under control, I'd be fast asleep in my Brooklyn apartment right about now. Actually...I glanced at the rising sun pouring across the Manhattan rooftops. I'd be waking up for another day in the office.

I didn't really miss that last part.

"How about a chamomile tea?" Valac asked, making me jump. I'd almost forgotten he was standing there waiting for me to say something. I was *that* bone tired.

"Demons drink chamomile tea?" I arched a brow.

"No." He strode across the floor, his footsteps silent. How strange. "But Priyanka loves it. She keeps a stash in the cabinet."

"Oh, right." I followed him into the kitchen just off the main room. Unlike Az's place, this penthouse didn't have an open floor plan, but the kitchen was almost as large as the living room. A little more life and color filled this space. Yellow curtains hung on the windows, matching the tablecloth.

Valac pulled the tea out of a cabinet by the fridge

and got some water boiling. I perched on a stool beside the marbled island and dropped my chin onto my fisted hands. Valac didn't say much. The guy was like a tomb.

"Thanks for letting me stay here," I finally said, breaking the silence.

He pulled out a black mug from another cabinet. "No need to lie, Mia. I know you aren't happy to be here. You'd rather stay with Az."

I blinked. "Oh. Well, sure. All of that is true. But I'm still grateful you didn't slam the door in my face and tell me to go sleep in a dumpster somewhere. That would have sucked."

Valac carried the mug over to the island and slid it toward me. He perched on the stool across from mine and shot me a twisted smile. "I follow orders."

"Just not Lucifer's, right? When did you decide to join Az's Legion?" I blew on the hot tea and took a timid sip. The liquid nearly scalded my tongue, but it soothed me all the same, filling my belly with heat.

He stood and pushed away from the island. "I know you find me strange, Mia. There's no need to have polite chitchat with me."

My mouth dropped open, and then I snapped it shut. How was I supposed to reply to that? Truth was...I *did* find him strange. Extremely so. Surely he knew how he came across? Until now, I didn't think he really cared.

"Don't push me away, Valac," I called after him.

He paused when he reached the door. Glancing over his shoulder, he arched his pale brow. "Push you away?"

"I can see what you're doing. I've done it myself." I took another sip of tea. "And that's why it won't work. We're friends now, and unfortunately, that means you're stuck with me."

He gave me a blank stare. "I know how you feel about me. I can read it clear as day. Are you going to tell me I'm wrong?"

"Of course not." I shrugged. "I do find you strange, but that doesn't mean I don't like you. In fact, being normal is overrated as far as I'm concerned."

He continued to give me that blank, unnerving stare. After a long moment, he glided over to the stool and rejoined me at the island. His bleached white hair fell into his eyes, but he didn't bother to brush it aside. "You're a very strange human."

Pain lanced through my heart. "Well, I'm not sure that's true. A lot of people seem to think that I'm not human at all."

"Hmm." His soul-shattering gaze swept across me. "It *is* very odd. I've heard nothing else quite like it."

"Do you think it's true?" I asked him, holding my breath. Even though the Legion was as clueless about this as I was, I desperately wanted to know what they thought. Maybe one of them had an explanation, something that made sense. A way that

85

none of it could be true...maybe then I wouldn't feel like the earth itself had been ripped out from under me.

"I believe you are *something*, but I can't say I have any clue what that something is. When I try to read your origins, it's like a void of nothingness."

I loosed my desperate breath. A void of nothingness. That definitely didn't make me feel any better about this.

"The truth is, Mia..." Valac suddenly gripped my hand. The tension in his fingers shot my veins with fear. "We have to convince Lucifer that you aren't who he thinks you are. I know Az didn't tell you, but Michael and Rafael are back to their old tricks. In the past week, there's been another two murders, just like the last time the angels were here. As long as Lucifer is around, we can do nothing to stop them." He leaned forward, his voice a harsh whisper. "Get him to leave. Satisfy his curiosity. Make him believe you're a werewolf. Do you understand what I'm asking of you?"

Dread shuddered through me. I lifted the mug to my lips and gulped down the tea, desperately wishing it was spiked with gin. This was not a good conversation to have sober. It felt like the future of everything rested on my shoulders, and I didn't have the strength to support the weight of it. How could I do anything other than crumble when pitted against Lucifer?

The literal King of Hell.

"That's a big ask," I whispered.

"I know." His eyes pierced my soul.

"How am I even supposed to do something like this?"

"One day at a time." He paused. "One fight at a time. Remember?"

The Legion's motto. Their rallying cry. I nodded, trying to find the courage within myself. It was a big mission, but this was a big, beautiful world with lots of beautiful people in it. There was so much more at stake than my own safety.

I clutched the mug. "One fight at a time."

9

S leep was a fickle beast, especially when the
fate of the world weighed on your mind. I
got maybe two hours tops before I threw off
the heavy comforter and padded into the kitchen,
still wearing the slinky dress from the night before.
It wasn't like I'd had a chance to pack my clothes. I
didn't even own pajamas right now.

Priyanka's brows shot to the top of her head
when I joined her at the kitchen table. She sat with
an open laptop perched next to a bowl of cereal,
scrolling through the news. My stomach rumbled.

"Fancy seeing you here." She pulled out the
chair beside her, the wooden feet scraping the stone
floor. "Sit. Tell me what's going on."

I plopped into the chair and sagged, still blind-
ingly weary. "Valac didn't tell you?"

"He's not the best communicator, if you haven't
figured that out yet."

89

So I filled her in. Every gory detail. Thankfully, she already knew most of the story. When I'd finished spilling my guts, she gave me a pat on the back and sighed.

"Az was right. The best option was to bring you here. Smart move."

"Is it?" My mind was so frazzled, I couldn't tell anymore. "Won't Lucifer wonder why I don't have a place of my own?"

She shook her head and dropped her spoon into her bowl. "You're not getting it. Lucifer already suspects you're Mia McNally. He's going to see if you slip up. It's a game. He loves a game. He's like us fae in that respect."

"And if I win, he'll go away?" I asked, my voice hitching.

"Maybe, if you make all the right moves." She winced. "It's not guaranteed, though, to be brutally honest. It depends on why he wants what he wants. If he's the one behind your fallen angel scent, there might be more going on than any of us realize. And when he gets bored of the game, he might finish what he started."

I shuddered, my heart twisting. "Finish what he started. So, like, *kill me*."

"Nope. He wants to marry you."

"And then I would become the Queen of Hell," I said in a tight voice.

"Exactly."

She said it so matter-of-factly, like it wasn't the

most terrifying thing I'd ever heard in my life. The Queen of Hell. What did that even mean? Would I have to sit on a throne engulfed in flames? And, for the millionth time, *why*? I hated being so far in the dark I couldn't even see my hand in front of my face.

Suddenly, Hendrix swooped in from the ceiling. There was a small balcony just outside the open sliding glass doors where an empty bowl sat on top of a wrought-iron table. Snacks, no doubt left for my pigeon. Who had done that? Az? Fondness curled around my heart as I reached out and rustled Hendrix's feathers. He cooed happily, leaning against my palm.

"Hi, Hendrix. Thanks for coming on this crazy journey with me."

Priyanka gave me an odd look and went back to her breakfast. We sat there for a while in silence. Me, petting Hendrix. Priyanka, scrolling through the news. It almost felt normal. It was a much-needed respite in the midst of so much insanity.

"Can you explain something to me, Priyanka?" I asked, turning back toward my new roommate.

After taking another crunchy bite of her cereal, she nodded. "I'll do my best."

"What's the difference between a fallen angel and a demon?" I crossed my legs and leaned back in the rickety chair. "I thought they were the same thing."

"Ah." She finished her cereal, pushing the bowl

away. "No, humans have that whole part wrong. Angels and demons are entirely different species from each other. They live in the realm of the afterlife. And they've been at odds for centuries, playing the game for souls."

"And fallen angels are...?"

"Angels who end up here. They've either abandoned their realm or have been kicked out of it for breaking the rules." She palmed the table and leaned forward. "I know why you're asking this. You're wondering if it's even possible that you're one of them. As crazy as it sounds, it is. If your parents were two fallen angels, you could have been born here, same as everyone else."

"My parents are definitely not fallen angels," I said with a bitter laugh. "Trust me."

Her brow arched. "No offense, but how do you know? Would you be able to tell? It sounds like things have been kept hidden from you. Maybe they were a part of that."

The question caught me off guard. Obviously, nothing about my parents even *suggested* they were fallen angels. My mother was an alcoholic, and my father had been absent for most of my life, always off on another business trip. My grades had never been good enough for either of them. My failed attempt at running track had put disappointment into their eyes. I'd succeeded at dancing, but they didn't like how much time I had dedicated to it. *It's sinful, moving that way*, my mother had often said.

And yet she drank herself unconscious multiple nights a week.

"They're nothing like the fallen angels I've met," I said, thinking of Suriel and Rafael. Those two were opposite sides of a coin, but still very much the same coin. There was nothing human about either of them, and it showed.

"Maybe someone hid them like they hid you."

"Maybe," I murmured, frowning.

Just as I opened my mouth to ask another question, Az strode into the kitchen. Caught off guard, my cheeks flushed with heat. Like always, he looked impossibly impeccable. His smooth dark suit highlighted his muscular physique, and the stubble scattered across his jawline was trimmed and neat. There were no bags beneath his eyes. No sagging shoulders. He looked ready to take on the world.

Me, meanwhile...well, I was a fucking mess.

"You're not ready to go?" he asked me, forgoing any pleasantries, just like always.

I simmered beneath his gaze. "Go where?"

"I see." He sighed. "Valac didn't tell you."

"There you go." Priyanka took a sip of her coffee. "Valac strikes again with his communication issues."

Az's eyes darkened. "We have an appointment at nine, and we can't be late." His gaze swept across my face. I hadn't removed my makeup last night, and I could feel the mascara clumped to my

JENNA WOLFHART

lids. Lovely. "How quickly can you be ready to go?"

I motioned at the sequinned dress. "Um, never? I'm not wearing this, and I don't have any other clothes here."

He frowned. "We don't have time to go shopping."

Priyanka pushed up from the table, tossing Hendrix a piece of her cereal. He caught it midair with a little flick of his tail feathers. "You can borrow something of mine. Come on, let's get you ready to go."

Stubbornly, I didn't move an inch. "No one has even told me where I'm going."

Much to the shock of no one, Az merely smiled as Priyanka bustled me out of the kitchen, keeping the information to himself. *Ugh. Demons.*

❀

We stood in the glittering, golden lobby of Parkins, Weller, and Smith while a fresh-faced receptionist murmured into a phone. Az stood tall beside me while my borrowed clothes hung oddly on my body. My damp hair curled around my shoulders, frizzed by New York's summer heat. There hadn't been time for me to use a hairdryer.

Serena bustled into the lobby in her pristine pantsuit and heels. Her shoes clicked along the

94

floor, echoing in the silence. When she reached us, she held out a hand. "Good morning, Mr. Asmodeus."

I bit back a laugh. *Mister Asmodeus?* Oh, he would never hear the end of this one.

"Good morning, Miss Mason." They shared a firm handshake, and nothing in either of their eyes indicated they were at all acquainted. Let alone that he'd saved her from a psychotic, supernatural serial killer. Serena had kept that little adventure under wraps. The partners of the firm frowned upon their attorneys getting involved in supernatural affairs outside of the office. That meant accidentally dating one and then being used as a lure.

For me.

And, rumor had it, I wasn't their favorite person on the planet.

"This is my assistant," Az said, turning toward me with a smile. It might have been convincing if he didn't look ready to growl at me. "Sansa."

"*Sansa?*" Her eyes bugged out of her head as she momentarily forgot herself. I winced. Serena was the reason I'd blurted out the name in the first place. Her obsession with those books had wormed its way into my head. Quickly, she recovered, pressing down on the front of her suit with nervous fingers. But when she spoke, she did so through gritted teeth. "Beautiful name. I wonder where I've heard it before. It sounds so familiar."

"Nowhere," I quipped. "It's pretty rare."

A low rumble sounded from Az's throat. "Miss Mason, my assistant and I need to do some research into the demon contracts your firm has on file. The request comes from Lucifer himself."

Lies.

Serena dropped her voice to a whisper. "You know, I'm really supposed to contact him and confirm that."

"I am Asmodeus," he said with a dangerous smile. "The First Prince of Hell. That's all the confirmation you need."

She glanced over her shoulder. The receptionist was engrossed in her phone call, and no one else was in the lobby. With a tsking noise, Serena turned back to us and nodded.

"If anyone asks, I contacted him," she warned. "People have been fired here for way less."

"Thanks, Serena," I mouthed back. "Winter is coming."

Shaking her head, she motioned for us to follow her through a pair of glass doors. Our shoes tapped against the marble floor, the echo like thunder in my ears. Or maybe that was my heart. It was throbbing against my ribs like a fist. I was way more nervous than the situation called for. We were here to look through the demon contracts. Totally fine. Totally legal. Totally not dangerous.

Mostly.

Serena led us into a small meeting room enclosed on all sides by more clear glass. As we settled around the table, she bustled from the room, returning moments later with a towering stack of paperwork. She plopped it onto the table before us and backed away. Her eyes were wild, like they sometimes got just before she shifted into a wolf.

"Don't take too long, all right?" she hissed through her teeth. "I really don't want to get fired."

She had fought tooth and nail for this job. Even in middle school, she'd wanted to work at a law firm in New York City. At the time, I hadn't known it was *this* one and what it meant. Parkins, Weller, and Smith specialized in supernatural legal issues. And Serena had worked her ass off to end up exactly here.

And now she was risking it all to help us find answers about my past. Hopefully, it would also give us a hint about Lucifer's involvement in all of this. The more we knew, the better we could beat him at his own game.

Az had filled me in on his plan during the drive here. The law firm kept records of the contracts between demons and humans, particularly when the deal resulted in the loss of a soul. Or a win, depending on which way you looked at it. Az believed a demon was behind my apparent memory loss when it came to the fallen angel scent. If that were true, there might be a contract with my name on it.

"You take that stack." Az shoved a pile of

contracts toward my side of the table. "And I'll take this one."

I nodded and flipped open the first file. "Do you really think we'll find answers here? If Lucifer is involved in this, would he have left behind a trail of evidence?"

"Lucifer loves paperwork. It helps him keep a running tally of souls." Az scanned the first file and then tossed it onto the left side of the table. He opened the next file and did the same with it. "This is my 'no' pile. Are you going to help?"

I hadn't even looked at the name on the first contract. My mind was too fried to focus. Az was acting like this was just a normal, everyday trip to a supernatural law firm when it was anything but. We were trying to find out if I was *a fallen angel whose memories had been wiped clean by the King of Hell*.

I couldn't even wrap my mind around it.

"I don't understand why he needs contracts," I continued, ignoring him. "Isn't there, like, a magical tally somewhere?"

His lips quirked. "We're demons, Mia. That doesn't mean everything we do is magic."

My name curled across his tongue. Shivers stormed down my spine. The heavy look in his eyes took me back to that night. His chest against mine. His lips between my thighs. Everything about it had felt so right, even though it had been so terribly wrong. Even if he'd been pretending.

"Relax." He reached under the table and palmed my knee. Heat shot through my core. "You look tense and on edge. If any of the partners walk by, they'll wonder why you look like a deer in headlights."

I swallowed hard. "How? I'm not okay, Az."

Although I was pretty okay with his hand on my knee.

Okay, *more* than just okay.

"Pretend," he murmured, leaning so close our foreheads touched. "You remember how to do that, don't you?"

"Yes." My voice came out raspy, like the very obvious idiot I was. But maybe he'd just think it was part of our new show, which was...pretending again, apparently. Fine with me. I didn't mind. In fact, I more than enjoyed it.

"Good." His lips curled as his scent consumed me. Fire and smoke. It filled my head until that was all I could focus on. Az. Me. The flames. His eyes darkened as his lips brushed my cheek. Everything within me tightened. Need clenched my thighs, so thick I ached.

I shuddered against him, letting go of my inhibitions. Our lips came so close that I could practically taste the toothpaste on his tongue.

And then he pulled back, leaving me a panting mess.

"I can't get your scent on me," he said, his voice going hard. "Lucifer would smell it the second he saw either of us. We can pretend to be a couple without touching."

"Oh." Disappointed, I slumped back in my chair. That had been a nice distraction, dammit. "Wait a minute. Why are we pretending to be a couple in Serena's law firm?"

He turned his eyes to the next contract, ignoring my question. His gaze pierced the page, and he crumpled the paper in his fists. "I've found you."

I gasped and leaned forward. "Seriously?"

"It doesn't help." With a growl, he tossed the contract onto my side of the table. My name was clearly at the top, along with an address in Hell's Kitchen. Everything else had been scribbled out with black marker. I let out a shuddering breath. The answers were here on this page, I was sure of it. But any important information had been stripped away.

Slowly, I lifted my gaze to meet his. That familiar look was in his eyes again. The one that made it clear he planned to rip off someone's head. And I had a pretty good idea whose head it was.

"What does this mean?" I dared to ask.

"Someone made it here first." He shoved back his chair, stood, and offered me his hand. "We can ask Serena, but I already know what she'll say. There will be no record of anyone else being here."

"Lucifer dropped in to look at the contracts," I said, shifting uneasily on the chair. "Serena mentioned it to me a couple of weeks ago."

Az's jaw clenched. "Of course he did."

"So that's it?" I motioned at the pile of contracts before us. "We've only looked through a dozen or so. Maybe there's more somewhere else."

"No, that's the one we needed. The answers are there, Mia. We just can't see them." He shoved his finger at the address left unmarked. "That's the only lead we have. We have to go there. Now."

10

T he car rumbled down the street. Az's driver was silent and still, just like always. He didn't even give us a curious glance when Az barked out his orders. Drive quickly. Avoid any traffic. Watch out for black wings in the sky.

My heart thumped as Az bit his knuckle and glared out the tinted windows. He was acting pretty freaked out, which wasn't doing much to make me feel better about this little plan of his.

"Az," I said softly. He jumped. "Do you think maybe it's a bad idea to go to this address? If Lucifer..." I glanced at the driver, who had zero reaction to my words. "If he messed with the contract, I doubt he would have left that address untouched without a reason. Maybe he's trying to lure us there."

"That's exactly what he's trying to do," Az said

in a hard voice.

I frowned. "Okay. Then maybe we shouldn't go there."

"We have to." He caught my hand in his and brought it to his chest. His heart pounded against my fingers. "There's something there. We need to know what it is."

"Except...that means we're walking straight into a trap. I don't know about you, but I think that's maybe a bad idea."

"Don't worry. We'll stay out of sight where he can't see us."

I pressed my lips together. "You're very determined to go through with this."

"I am." He dragged his gaze from the window and met my eyes. Flames roared within them, and shadows whispered across his skin. "He's destroyed all the other evidence. This might be our only chance to find out the truth. What you are. What was done to you."

Pain ripped through me. My eyes slid shut. "I don't know if it's worth it then. Maybe it's better if I never find out."

A beat passed before he answered. "Surely you don't mean that."

"I don't know, Az." I flipped open my eyes to meet his dark gaze again. "How would you feel if you were me? My entire life might be a lie, and it terrifies me. It has something to do with Lucifer and Hell and fallen angels. Magic and hidden scents and fae glamor. Do you know how crazy that sounds to me? I'm a human. That's all I've ever known. This is all just way too much for me to handle."

"But it's *not* all you've never known." His voice softened, and the shadows blinked away. Now it was just me and him. "Unlike most humans, you've been aware of the supernatural world for most of your life. You accepted it. You understand it. And when I came into your life, instead of screaming into my face, you..." He cleared his throat and glanced away. "The Legion noticed it in you. So did our dancers. You seem to fit, Mia."

Fit. He put words to the feeling I'd had for weeks, something I thought I might have only imagined. In just a few short weeks, I'd felt like I belonged at *Infernal* with the magic, the demons, and the fae. My best friend was even a werewolf. The supernatural world felt like home.

I sucked in a rattling breath as the realization washed over me. At the time, I hadn't thought much of it. I'd spent so long bobbing along in a sea of solitude that it'd made sense I'd grasp on to the first group of people who welcomed me into their lives with open arms. Even if they were Princes of Hell.

But maybe there was more to it than that. Maybe I'd felt like I fit in with a bunch of supernaturals because...I was one myself.

Could that *really* be the case?

We were about to find out. Maybe. Az seemed

certain we would find answers at this address, but I had a sneaking suspicion we'd just find Lucifer lurking in the shadows and waiting for us to walk straight into his trap.

The driver angled the car toward the curb and left the engine running. Peering out the tinted windows, I tried to steel myself for what we were about to do. But, to be honest, my entire body felt a little wobbly. What was it people said? Bravery isn't the lack of fear. It's doing the thing you fear even if it liquidates your bones.

Az slid out of the car, rounded the back, and swung the door open for me to climb out. I put one booted foot on the sidewalk and braced myself for the inevitable swoop of black wings. But nothing came. People bustled by, heads down. It was the middle of the day on a busy Manhattan street, and Lucifer was nowhere to be seen.

I glanced up at the number on the building in front of us while Az slammed the car door. Twenty-six. The address we were looking for was forty-eight, unless I'd totally missed the mark here. And that was always a possibility.

"The building is on the other side of this block." Az took my elbow and led me toward the revolving doors. "We're going to approach it through this one and stay out of sight until we're sure he isn't in there."

"But he *is* going to be in there," I said, glancing up at him. "Isn't he?"

Az nodded. "Most likely."

"I still think this is a terrible idea."

"We need to see what he wants us to see." Az led us to the revolving doors, and we pushed against the golden frame. "We just can't let *him* see *us*."

I rolled my eyes. Demons were so weird. "But he knows we're going to follow this trail, right? So what makes you think he won't spot us? Or smell us? He's big on the whole scent thing, right?"

"We'll stay well out of sight."

I sighed. There really was no talking him out of this. A part of me wasn't sure I even *wanted* to know the truth. If the fae was right and I was a fallen angel, what would that mean for my future? Would that make me an enemy to Az? Could angels and demons date?

Not that we were dating anyway, I had to remind myself. We'd had a very brief, fake fling, and he'd shown little interest in me since he'd dropped me in that Brooklyn apartment and walked out of my life.

I refused to spend the rest of my life pining after a guy who wasn't interested.

The rest of my life. My gut twisted. Wait a minute. Was I *immortal*?

We strode through a dimly-lit lobby and passed a bank of grungy elevators where a few people stood waiting. They glanced at us as we passed but went back to their phones with disinterest. One person wore a full-on bunny costume, complete with an oversized, floppy-eared head.

It wasn't the strangest thing I'd ever seen in Manhattan.

"You seem to know where you're going," I whispered to Az when I felt sure we were well out of earshot.

His lips tipped up in the corners. A dimple briefly made an appearance. "The Legion and I have lived in Hell's Kitchen for a very long time. Stolas spent the past decade making us a map of every building."

I arched a brow. "An entire decade?"

"Sometimes, good work takes time."

"Must be one hell of a map," I muttered.

It didn't surprise me one bit that Stolas was the demon behind it. Unlike Caim and Phenex, he rarely cracked a smile or seemed drawn to chaos. I could easily picture him with his head down, bent over a massive canvas and drawing tiny details for hours.

We reached the back wall and hung a left down a corridor lit only by a flickering fluorescent bulb. It buzzed like bees as we passed beneath it. A few doors down, Az twisted a knob and pushed inside an empty room. A stairwell sat to our left. We jogged up two flights and entered another vacant room that looked out onto an alley.

"That's the building." Az pointed at a red-brick walk-up that squatted on the opposite side of the alley. Dozens of windows stared back at us, some covered in blinds or curtains. A few windows were bare, and we could clearly see residents wandering around their apartments. Some cooked. Some watched TV. One girl was petting her cat.

I shifted on my feet. "Um, this feels a bit voyeuristic."

Az crossed the room and stood before the large window. I hissed and latched onto his arm, trying to drag him back. But he was like a stone statue. Immovable and...whoops. I could feel his muscles tense beneath my fingers. My god, his biceps were sculpted to perfection. I wanted to run my fingers over them and—

I dropped my hands and backed away.

He shot me a wicked smile. "You're worried someone will see you in here with me."

"Um. Yes. That someone is *Lucifer*."

"The windows in this building are tinted. That's why I chose this one." He pointed out the dark film on the outer glass. "If anyone looks into this room, they'll see vague shadowy forms and nothing more."

"Oh." Relaxing a little, I stepped up beside him. No wonder it had taken Stolas so long to plot out his map of Hell's Kitchen. He'd even nailed down details about which buildings had tinted glass and which did not. "So what exactly are we looking at? Is one of these windows in the apartment from that contract?"

My contract. Had I signed it? I certainly didn't remember doing anything of the sort.

"I'm not sure." Az folded his arms, standing tall and firm beside me. For a moment, I let my eyes wander across his body. His corded muscles tensed as he gazed at the building across from us. That strong, unyielding jawline rippled with determination. *Why* did he have to be so damn hot?

His lips curled. "Have you forgotten that I can scent your emotions, Mia?"

Alarm rippled through me, and I jerked my gaze away. Heat consumed my face until I was sure it was actually on fire. To be honest, I kind of had forgotten. Not that it would have made any difference. I couldn't control how I felt any more than any other living, breathing human with eyes. He was sexy as sin. It was just a fact. If he had a Wikipedia page, it would be one of the first things listed about him.

"You sure do like to jump to conclusions," I said with a mouthful of marbles. Time to save a little face, if even possible. "Whatever you think you smell, you're wrong. It doesn't mean what you think it means."

"If you say so." He chuckled.

My eyes narrowed. "You have a massive ego. Pretty rich coming from the most anno—"

"There he is." The smile slipped from Az's face. He took one step closer to the window and pointed up at an apartment two floors above us.

Heart pulsing, I followed the line of his finger. Az was right. There he was. Lucifer's silver hair flashed beneath the sunlight streaming in through the window. His hands were wrapped around an old man's throat.

I sucked in a sharp gasp.

Everything happened in the blink of an eye. Lucifer smiled. He stepped up closer to the window and snapped the man's neck in one fluid motion.

Horror tumbled through me.

I screamed.

Lucifer whirled toward our building, his eyes scanning the windows. Az grabbed my arm and pulled me toward the door. I stumbled after him, reaching up to touch my cheeks. They were wet with tears.

When we reached the door, I shot one last glance over my shoulder. Lucifer was gone from the window now. Had he seen us? The glass was tinted, but he'd still be able to make out our forms. Would he have recognized the shape of us?

Az didn't wait around to find out. He grabbed my hand and hurtled up the stairwell. Our footsteps echoed through the concrete space like war drums. When we reached the rooftop, he gathered me into his arms and shot up into the clouds on his wings of darkness.

But it was far too late. I knew Lucifer had heard my scream.

11

Az set down on a rooftop only a few blocks away. He hadn't wanted to remain in the sky for long to avoid Lucifer—or humans —spotting us. He'd found a roof that held a maze of concrete structures for us to hide among, but it all felt a bit pointless to me. If Lucifer really wanted to find us, wouldn't he?

Fisting his hands, Az paced before me. Tension rattled his body, and a strange, sizzling heat seemed to waft off his skin. I'd never seen him like this before. Like he was just as shaken as I was by what we'd seen.

"Why are we here?" I asked. "Won't he know exactly where we are because of his smell tracking thing?"

Az shook his head. "That's not how it works. He has to be actively tracking someone to keep his sights on them. Once he focuses on something else, he loses that connection, though he can pick it up again if they get near enough."

"Near enough," I said flatly. "Like we just did."

"That was a big building with a lot of people. Besides, we weren't actually that close to him. There were two walls between us and several stories," Az said, ruffling his dark locks. "As powerful as he is, he isn't infallible."

"So we're safe?" I asked with a hopeful hitch in my voice.

"No."

The ground fell out from beneath my feet. "Oh."

Az shot me a sharp glance. There must have been something in my voice that gave away my fear. Not that he'd have to be a mind reader to get it. I knew I was visibly terrified.

Suddenly, he was beside me so quickly that it was as if he'd moved through time itself. He gathered me into his arms and pulled me against his chest. His heartbeat thundered against my ear.

I knew he was trying to help me relax, but nothing about this soothed me. All I could think about was his lips near my cheek and his muscles hard against my breasts.

"I'm sorry you had to see that, Mia," he murmured, his breath tickling my neck. "I had no idea you'd have to see something like that."

Unshed tears flooded my eyes. I'd seen a lot of terrible things in the past couple of months, but nothing quite like this. The King of Hell had snapped an old man's neck right in front of me, and he'd wanted me to see it. It was all part of his game. One clearly meant to terrorize me.

Sniffling, I pulled back to search Az's eyes for answers I knew he didn't have. "Why did he do that? What is all of this about, Az? We keep trying to find answers, but it makes less and less sense."

"I don't know, Mia." He palmed my cheek, dropping his forehead to mine. "Did you know that man?"

I shook my head. I'd never seen him before in my life. He couldn't have been younger than eighty, and while his salty hair reminded me of my own grandfather's, they shared no other resemblance. Grandpa Martin was at least six feet tall, and he had wide shoulders and a sly smile. The victim in the window had been a slight, wiry man with glasses.

Now that I'd had a moment to process what we'd seen, I couldn't get past the strangest part of it. The man hadn't looked scared at all. Resigned, maybe. Like he'd expected this to happen. Maybe he had.

"Could he have been a demon, Az?" I asked. "Maybe I signed the contract with him, and he was the one who wiped my memories."

"Demons don't age. Not once they're fully grown."

"Oh, right." I flushed as the hand on my cheek slid down to my shoulder. Even as we spoke about demon contracts and forgotten memories, I was

115

hyperaware of his every move. "What does all this mean then? What do we do now?"

This had been our only lead. The only hope we had of finding answers. Tears trailed down my cheeks. There was something wrong with me, and no one could tell me what it was. No one except for the most powerful demon in the world. The one who wanted to steal me away to the underworld.

I just felt so lost, like an essential part of myself was vanishing into the past. Mia McNally, the dancer, the pigeon lover. My mortal life had been next to impossible the past few years, but at least it had been mine. Who was I if I wasn't *me*?

Az gently wiped my cheeks with his knuckles. Embarrassed, I tried to pull away, but he held me firmly in his arms. The warmth of him flooded my senses, chasing away the fear and pain.

"I'm going to kill him," he muttered, pulling me against his powerful chest.

"I thought you couldn't kill a demon," I whispered back.

"Yeah, well." Anger rumbled from his throat. "I'll do the next best thing. Rip out his heart and bury it on the other side of the earth."

Chills swept down my arms. His viciousness *should* scare me, but it did the opposite. It made me feel safer than I ever had. As far as I was concerned, if he ripped out Lucifer's heart, he'd be doing the entire world a massive favor.

"He doesn't get to make you feel like this," he

continued, his voice rumbling against my ear. "I won't allow it."

I tipped back my head to stare up into his tense face. "What would happen if you *did* decide to fight him? He's the one in charge, isn't he? I'll admit, I know next to nothing about Hell, but he's the King. Can't he make you return to Hell if you try to go against him?"

He nodded, his jaw rippling with tension. "He can order us to return to Hell anytime he wants. But as powerful as he is, we could try to resist him..."

He didn't sound particularly convinced.

"We'll have to wait for the right moment," he continued, his gaze growing distant. "We need to act as normally as possible. Pretend that we're still playing along with his game. And then when the moment comes, the Legion and I will destroy him. I will never let him get his hands on you. Do you understand me?"

I shivered and dropped my voice to a whisper. "What happens when someone destroys the King of Hell?"

"The next in line takes the throne."

"But that's you." I palmed his chest and stepped back. Horror and confusion and hope tangled together in my gut until I didn't know where one emotion ended and the other began. "Does that mean you'd have to leave Manhattan? What about the game for souls? What happens then, Az?"

"It's the only way, Mia," he murmured, capturing my eyes with those flaming shards.

"No, it isn't," I said, my hands fisting. "Only this morning, we decided the way forward was to play the game and convince Lucifer that I'm not a problem. Right? And then he would go on his merry way back to Hell. Why can't we go with that one? Why do you have to pick the most *extreme* option that's available?"

"Mia." He took my hand and tugged me back to him. "You aren't understanding what we just witnessed."

"Oh, I'm understanding it. Lucifer just killed maybe the only person alive who knows what was in that contract."

"Yes. And no." His lips flatlined. "He left the address visible for us to see. So that we would follow him there. It was a message, Mia. Going against him is futile. He will do whatever it takes to win."

I closed my eyes. "So Priyanka was right. He'll never give up, will he?"

"He won't give up until he gets what he wants," Az said in a dangerous voice. "And that thing is Mia McNally as his bride. I will never let that happen. He will have to rip my limbs off my body and scatter them around the far ends of the world before I will let him lay a single hand on you."

Pain pounded out a rhythm in my heart. More tears leaked out of my eyes. I couldn't stop them. If only I had just ignored my damn curiosity, Lucifer might have left Manhattan in a week or two. He never would have caught my scent. I'd be safe. The Legion would be safe. None of this would have happened. "I fucked up."

Az cupped my cheeks with his palms, and his dark gaze bored into my soul. "No. I won't let you blame yourself for this."

"But it's my fault, and we both know it. If you die trying to protect me, I'll never be able to live with myself."

"I'm never going to die," he said roughly. "It's impossible."

"He could still destroy you," I whispered, hating even the sound of those words. It seemed impossible. Az, gone from this world. But he wasn't indestructible even if he was immortal. The same method he wanted to use against Lucifer could be used against him, too. He'd lost one of his demons just like this.

"I am stronger than you think I am. Just because I haven't shown you the full extent of my powers doesn't mean they aren't there." His palm swept down the side of me before resting on my hips. "Trust me, Mia. I am one hell of a force to be reckoned with."

My chest burned as I stared into his eyes. That *zing* went through me once again, and a sudden burst of shadowy memories rushed through my mind. Too fast for me to comprehend them. And then they were gone.

What was that all about?

Confusion rippled through me as I leaned toward Az. I felt inexplicably drawn to him more than I ever had. Maybe it was the fear and the adrenaline. Maybe it was the danger in his voice when he spoke of stopping Lucifer from ever getting his hands on me. Or maybe it had something to do with that weird *zing*.

"Az, do you feel that?" I whispered to him.

He searched my eyes with his. "Feel what?"

"That weird feeling. Like a bolt of electricity or something..." I trailed off, realizing how ridiculous those words sounded out loud. *A weird blast of electricity? Really, Mia.* It was probably just my raging hormones.

A strange expression whispered across his face. "Interesting."

Interesting? Yep, definitely not the response I'd been hoping for.

"I know it's ridiculous. Just ignore what I—"

His mouth claimed mine, shutting down whatever nonsense I'd been about to say next. A thrill shot through my core, and heat enveloped me. Desperate desire rose within me as I pushed up onto my toes and wound my arms around his neck. A low growl rumbled in the back of his throat. Animalistic and urgent.

Everything fell away as his lips tore through me

with hunger. I clung onto him, my need ripping through me like a hurricane. His hands palmed my ass and tugged me close. Our bodies melted together, forming one.

Questions popped into my head that I tried to ignore. What did this mean? Had he missed me the way I'd missed him? Did this mean our night together had actually meant something to him?

Pesky thoughts. None of that really mattered right now. One hand slipped between my thighs, and sparks lit up my entire body. I shuddered as his fingers brushed my jeans. My legs squeezed tight around him, and a moan slipped from my throat.

Stumbling, my back slammed against the concrete block behind me. I reached between us to unbutton my jeans. I didn't care where we were or who was after us. A hot, desperate ache tore through my core. I was going to explode.

Suddenly, he pulled back and shook his head like he was trying to get water out of his ears. A gulf of cold air roared between us, erasing the heat. Disappointment fell like an anchor in my gut. My hands dropped to my sides, and I forced my heaving chest to calm the hell down.

"He'll smell you on me," he said, fisting his hands.

"I don't care," I shot back. Because I very much didn't. Not right now.

"It isn't safe." He took another step away from

me. "And I won't do anything to jeopardize your safety."

"You keep saying that." I lifted my chin and stalked toward him. "But don't you think it's my decision to make? Or is this just an excuse to push me away? *Again?*"

Turned out I was still a little angry that he'd plopped me in Brooklyn and ordered me to stay away from the only people who had ever accepted me for who and what I was, other than Serena. And to stay away from him when he'd known, deep down, that I'd wanted to see where this thing between us led.

Instead of answering me, his wings flared wide on either side of him. The sunlight glimmered against the deep black, filling out the lines of every feather. Power hummed from his body. The scent of ash swirled toward me like a puff of smoke. I was momentarily struck by the beauty of those wings. Mouth dropping, I stared.

Bad idea. I shouldn't have gotten distracted. Az took the opportunity to haul me into his arms and shoot off into the sky again.

12

Asmodeus took me straight to his penthouse. He strode through the open balcony doors with my body tucked against him like I was some kind of damsel in distress. With a roll of my eyes, I hopped out of his arms before he had a chance to put me down himself. I might be mostly human, but I wasn't helpless. Thank you very much.

"You seem annoyed again." Az shot me an irritated glance and tossed his keys onto the dining table. Not that he'd used them to get inside. For the second time in two days, we'd come by air.

"As far as I can tell, the feeling is mutual." I folded my arms and watched him pace around his apartment. He slammed the balcony doors shut and then threw heavy black curtains over them. After giving me another dark look, he stormed around,

123

pressing his hand to every wall like some kind of angry carpenter.

"What are you doing?"

"Checking to make sure Lucifer hasn't been here."

I arched my brows. "By petting the walls?"

He shot me a dark look. "I had a witch come over a couple of weeks ago and put some wards in place. If anyone steps over the boundary, the wards break. It's an alarm system."

"There are witches?" I shouldn't have been surprised. If magic existed—and it did—surely witches did, too. There were fae and vampires and demons. Might as well be magic-wielders to go along with them. Still, every time I learned something new about the supernatural world, it felt as though the world titled sideways just a little bit more. Soon, I'd be all the way upside down.

"A few. Most of the families didn't survive the 1600s, but they're growing again."

I filed that information away for later use. Might come in handy at some point. Witches were a thing, and they knew magic.

"So has anyone been here?" I asked, while Az spent a long time poking around the door that led to the rest of the building.

"Not that I can tell," he muttered.

I fought the urge to roll my eyes. He was in a terrible mood, not that this was any different from his usual self. Just a tad more grumbly. It seemed our argument on the rooftop had set him off. Lucky for me that I had this effect on him.

"Okay." I stood in the center of his apartment, my hands hanging awkwardly by my thighs. "Why are we here, Az? You've been super focused on our scents not mixing, and they definitely will if I'm in your actual home. Besides, I thought you wanted me to stay with Valac."

"You will stay with Valac." He pushed away from the door and turned my way. "After today."

"Okay, so..." I wet my lips as he strode across the floor with a fiery heat in his eyes. Again, I asked him, "Why not today? Why are we here? Can you just stop being so mysterious and tell me what's going on?"

He stood tall before me and roughly cupped the back of my neck. Hunger roared through his eyes as his fingers tightened their grip on me. Need flared back to life in my core. I tipped back my head, my entire body tensing.

"I brought you here because I can't be around you any longer without ripping your goddamn clothes off. And if I'm going to fuck you the way I want, we can't be out in public. We need to be here in private where we can rinse our scents off each other when we're done."

Oh. *Oh.* I swallowed hard. My lips parted. I'd longed for him to say these words, but now that he had, I didn't know what the hell to do about it. Nerves tumbled through my belly. This time, we

JENNA WOLFHART

didn't have liquid courage as an excuse. This time, it felt far more real.

"Then do it," I whispered to him. "Fuck me, Az."

His hands palmed my ass, and he lifted me from the floor. My thighs stretched wide on either side of him, just as his lips claimed mine. Need pulsed within my core. Our kiss deepened with hunger, and his low growl rumbled through me.

His shoulders tensed beneath my fingers, his chiseled muscles rippling with strength. I slid my hand up his neck, tangling my fingers in his hair. It was as soft as the shadows that pulsed against his skin.

I revelled in the feel of him. During those long nights spent apart, he'd filled my dreams. But it had never been better than this. His arms, his hands, his mouth. The electric pulse that charged between us. There was nothing else in the world like this, and I hated that I'd spent so many nights without it.

A little voice popped up in the back of my head. There was a reason we'd parted ways, and it had to do with the pesky demon king trying to rip apart both our lives. We probably shouldn't be doing this. But the delicious thrill of forbidden desire shoved all those thoughts aside.

Az carried me across the room and slammed my back against the wall. His body humming, he unwound my thighs from his hips and flipped me around. A gasp popped from my throat when he

126

yanked my shirt over my head, leaving my breasts exposed to the cool, air-conditioned penthouse.

One hand snaked up my belly, teasing my breast, while he pinned my arms over my head with his other hand. A little thrill went through me. I kind of enjoyed being trapped like this. I gasped as he twisted my nipple hard.

He dropped his mouth to my ear and murmured, "You did a very bad thing, Mia. We made a deal, and you broke it."

"Oh." I flushed, biting my bottom lip. "I suppose I ought to be punished for it."

Nipping at my ear, he continued, "Normally, a demon would steal the soul of an oath-breaker. But we can't do that, now can we?"

"Sounds like you'll have to come up with something else." I glanced over my shoulder at him. "I have a few ideas."

He slipped his hand between my legs and unzipped my jeans. As his lips caressed my neck, I arched toward him, but his palm grasped my hips and pushed me back.

"We'll do things at my speed," he said with a laugh. "For your punishment."

"Sure. Okay. Punish me as long as you like." I gasped when he pushed down my jeans and then followed them with my lacy thong. I was now one hundred percent naked before him, and he was fully clothed. When I tried to reach behind me to unbutton his shirt, he tightened his grip on my wrists.

He flipped me around again so that I faced him. His hungry eyes tore across me, drinking in my body. Heart pounding, I wet my lips, tilting back my head so that he would kiss me.

A wicked smile played across his lips. He dropped his mouth to my breast and dragged his tongue across my nipple. Desire lit up my insides. Arching toward him, I moaned.

His lips stole across my chest to my other peaked nipple. Hand still trapping my wrists, he sucked hard. I shuddered as my core clenched tight. Heat built between my thighs, making me ache for him.

I was starting to feel like I might scream if he didn't do something more than just play with my breasts.

And I had a feeling that was the point.

"Okay," I whispered after another agonizing round of nipple teasing. "This feels amazing, but..."

"But what, Mia?" Laughter danced in his eyes, and his dimples made a rare appearance. He was enjoying this far too much.

"You know." I flushed. "There are some other parts of my body that might want a little attention."

"Might?" He arched a brow. "Hmm. *Only* might?"

"How about definitely?" I whispered.

His gaze dropped to my thighs. With a delicious,

panty-melting smile, he slid one finger down the length of me. He stopped just above my folds. Ice-blue eyes boring into me, he asked a silent question.

"Yes. Please." The ache was almost overwhelming. I could hardly think, let alone speak.

"You'll never break one of our deals again?" he asked in a growl.

"As long as you never make me sign another contract."

He chuckled and pulled back. "Mia."

"Az."

"You are infuriating."

I smiled up at him. "So are you."

He shifted closer to me, pressing his body against mine. I could feel the hardness of his cock through his pants, pressing into my pubic bone. We were playing a little game, one he wasn't necessarily winning. He wanted me just as much as I wanted him.

And then his eyes darkened. "You seem to have such little regard for your own safety. Can't you see I'm just trying to keep you safe? If anything happened to you, I'd..."

My heart pulsed. He'd what?

As he stared into my eyes, his grip on my arms relaxed. Slowly, I dropped my hands onto his shoulders and slid them down his shirt. My fingers made quick work of his buttons. I pushed the material back, revealing his sculpted chest.

He was perfect, every single inch of him. It was

as if someone had plucked the image of him from my head and made him just for me.

"Promise me you'll never break a deal with me again," he whispered.

"No." When he winced, I caught his chin between my fingers and kept his gaze on me. "No more deals. No more contracts. That doesn't mean I won't listen to you or agree to your plans. But I never want to sign my name along a dotted line again."

For a moment, I thought he'd keep arguing with me. Az was stubborn and set in his ways. I knew he used the contracts as a way to keep me safe, and he didn't want to let go of that. But then he dragged his thumb along my bottom lip and sighed.

"I can't say no to you." He kissed me, softer than before. Our lips melted together as our bodies collided against the wall. Lifting me from the floor again, he trapped me there with my breasts against his chest and my thighs around his waist.

He slid inside of me, lighting me up with every inch. I clutched his shoulders as he thrust deep inside. Need consumed me, driving away everything else. Instinctively, my thighs spread wider, eager for more.

"Fuck, Mia." He growled out my name as his thrusts went deeper. "How is it even possible you feel this good?"

I gasped as he slammed into me. Sweat beaded on my brow at the heat pouring off his body in waves. My climax built inside my core like a hurricane. He gripped my thighs, tugging my body toward his, and that was all it took to undo me completely.

I shattered around him, my orgasm stronger than any I'd ever had. A ringing filled my head as he followed quickly behind.

We clung to each other until our heartbeats slowed. Then gently, Az lowered me to the floor. I leaned against him and breathed him in, grateful for the scent of fire and smoke. I'd missed it.

"We need to shower," he said, rubbing my back. "As much as I want to bask in you for hours, I can't. If Lucifer caught us like this, it would all be over."

I sighed and nodded. "And so the bubble is burst."

"We can put it back together." He squeezed my shoulder as we padded into his master bathroom. "When Lucifer has returned to Hell, we can spend as much time as we'd like in this bedroom."

I tried not to read too much into it, but I couldn't help myself. He'd always been so closed off about his feelings. I hadn't even been sure he'd ever wanted me until now.

Lifting my eyes to his face, I braced myself to see his disinterest. But I didn't find it. Instead, all I found was heat. I gave him a sly smile. "And how much time would that be?"

"Hours. Days. Weeks." He traced his thumb along the skin beneath my ear, causing a fresh wave of shivers. "You are beautiful, Mia. Your little gasps when I touch you are the sexiest thing I've ever heard in my life."

With a little smile, I gasped.

"Yes," he growled. "Just like that."

"Do we really have to go now?"

He pulled open the door to his walk-in shower and turned on the tap. Water poured down from the ceiling like rainfall. "Well, we do need to shower before we leave. Might as well make it interesting."

My core tightened. Sounded good to me.

The moment I stepped inside *Infernal*, I half-expected Lucifer to look into my eyes and read everything that had happened between me and Az. We'd done our best to wash the scent off our bodies, but I felt as though the connection between us had been imprinted on my soul.

A bit melodramatic, really, but hey. Sometimes girls get crushes on demons and all logic flies right out the window. It didn't help that it had taken us a full two hours to get out of his penthouse. Every time we tried to leave, one of us got frisky. It had been one of the best days I'd had in the past few years. Too bad it came with the threat of Hell.

Much to my relief, Lucifer was nowhere to be seen. Az left me in the Legion's meeting room while he made his rounds before the club's doors opened. He was a perfectionist a lot of the time, at least when it came to his club. He liked to make sure everything was spic and span before his patrons arrived. Every chair in place. Every stain on the floor scrubbed. It needed to glisten and gleam for the night's party.

This place might be a front for some secret soul saving, but *Infernal* was still his baby.

"Mia!" Caim beamed and leaned back in his chair. "Come join us."

He sat with Stolas and Bael around the metal folding table. Playing cards were spread out before them. There was no sign of their map or the detailed files that tracked dangerous supernaturals working for Lucifer. Right now, they couldn't focus on any of that. Lucifer's presence in the club shut all that down.

"You should probably call me Sansa," I said as I dropped into the chair. "You never know when *you know who* could be lurking around. I'm not going to let him win that easily, especially after what happened today..."

I cut myself off, cheeks flushing. Might be best if I kept that information to myself.

"Lucifer is currently preoccupied." Caim snickered and flipped over one of the cards. A red king stared up at us. Bael whooped. Stolas scowled.

"Preoccupied how exactly?"

Stolas shot Bael and Caim a stern look. "These two talked Phenex into setting a little trap for him. The idiots. It's going to blow up in all of our faces."

My heart flipped. Uh oh. "Do I even want to know?"

Caim's eyes flickered with a wicked glint. He was always the more lighthearted, easygoing one of the bunch, but I couldn't forget he was a demon at heart. He had a wicked streak, just like the rest of them. He just never aimed that darkness at me.

"Phenex went to your old apartment and grabbed some clothes from your hamper." Stolas's expression darkened. "He brought them back here, waved them all around, and then took off toward the Brooklyn Bridge."

I sat up a little straighter. "You mean he stole my dirty laundry?"

Stolas held up his hands. "Sorry, Mia. It wasn't my idea."

Wrinkling my nose, I shook my head. "Okay, it's a little weird, but it's also not a bad plan. If he catches my old scent, maybe he'll stop suspecting I'm, well, me."

"Might be okay if they left it at that," Stolas grumbled.

Caim grinned. "Lucifer refuses to cross the East River. No one knows why, but I've got a hunch it's because it dims his powers somehow. So, we're dangling some bait in front of him. Some delicious bait. If he wants to get to you, he has to go on that bridge."

"And when he does, Phenex and Valac will destroy him," Bael said with a satisfied smile.

Dread dropped like a stone in my gut. "Wait. They're going to try to destroy him? *Now?* Az doesn't know about any of this, does he?"

"Ah." Caim winced. "Not yet. We were afraid he'd rush in there and try to do it himself. I've seen the expression on his face for the past couple of days. He's two seconds away from completely losing his shit."

"But you're his family. His Legion. He trusts you more than anyone."

"Exactly." Bael palmed the table and stood. The table groaned beneath him when he leaned forward to capture my eyes. "We will protect him with our lives."

I flushed, fear tumbling through me. I knew they were only trying to help, but Az wouldn't like this. Not one bit. If they were going to take on Lucifer, he'd want to be there. To protect his Legion, if anything. I couldn't bear to think how much it would hurt him if he lost another member of his family. Morax's death had almost destroyed him. I hadn't been there when it had happened, but he carried the remnants of that pain with him even now.

"This is a bad idea." As much as I loved these guys, I had to tell Az. "How long ago did they leave for the bridge?"

Caim cocked his head and smiled. "You actually care what happens to us, don't you?"

I threw up my hands and stood. "Of course I do,

you idiot. You six demons are my family now, too, whether you like it or not."

The words popped out of my mouth before I'd even had a chance to think them through. Family? These guys? The demons of Hell's Kitchen? But the truth of it hung heavily on my tongue. Sure, it had been an impulsive thing to say in the heat of the moment, but I'd meant every word. When I looked at these guys, they felt like home.

Maybe *that* was the real reason I was so desperate to stay in New York. It wasn't the city calling my name. It was the Legion.

No time to think about that now. Phenex and Valac had gone rogue, and I had to tell Az before they got themselves destroyed.

"Sorry," I told Caim. "But you know I have to tell him."

"Tell him what?" an eerie voice rang out from the open door.

Everything within me tensed. Bael sat hard on his chair and Caim winced. I did my level best to keep the panic off my face, but I knew my scent would be thick with it. My hands moved as if they had a mind of their own. Pulse tripping through my fingers, I flipped over the next card on the pile.

It was a ten of spades.

I let out a low whistle. "See, Stolas? Caim is cheating. That's the third time in a row he's had the perfect hand. Somehow, he's rigged the deck. I thought you'd want to know."

For a moment, no one said anything. Hopefully, no one took a close look at their hands. I had no idea how my brain had conjured that little story, but I hoped to hell the others would go along with it. Lucifer knew I hadn't been talking about cards when he'd walked through that door, but it didn't matter. This was all part of the game, I realized. He wanted to see how long it took before I cracked.

Well, he'd have to do a hell of a lot better than this.

"Hmm." Stolas tossed his cards onto the folding table. "Bit of a cheap trick, isn't it, Caim? Too scared to try and win on your own?"

Caim rolled his eyes and gave us a lazy smile, folding his arms as he leaned back in his chair. "Thought I'd see how long it took you two to figure it out. Turns out, I could have tricked you for weeks. Or maybe even longer. If it wasn't for Sansa here, you'd have never known."

"Sansa is very clever," Lucifer said in a purr. He strode toward me and twisted a strand of my hair around his finger. Jerking back my head, I fought the urge to spit in his face.

"Yeah, sure," Bael said, clearly uncomfortable. "Listen, Lucifer, mate. Want to join us for a game? We suddenly need another player since Caim here can't play straight."

"A little game sounds delicious." Lucifer leaned closer and sniffed my neck. My teeth ground together and my fingers formed claws. An overwhelming urge to punch him in the gut rushed through me.

Caim stood, and the chair toppled violently behind him. "Take my place then, Luc."

Lucifer's eyes slanted toward Caim, and his voice came out a hiss. "Is there some kind of problem? You all seem so very tense. Where are the rest of you, anyway? Shouldn't Phenex and Valac be here by now? Your little club opens soon."

He knew. Something had tipped him off. Or maybe he'd just been clever enough to put two and two together. Clearly he couldn't prove it, or this whole place would be up in flames by now. The Legion would be gone from earth, sent straight back to Hell.

And I'd be sitting beside Lucifer as his bride.

He didn't have proof, but *he knew*.

Caim shrugged. "Haven't seen them all day, but that's nothing to worry about. They'll be here by the time the doors open."

"Who cares where the others are?" Stolas growled. "Caim here has been cheating us for weeks. Do you know how much money I've lost to this asshole?"

Bael caught my eyes across the table, and he gave me an almost imperceptible nod. Somehow, I knew exactly what he was trying to tell me. *Get the hell out while you can.*

I cleared my throat and drifted toward the door. "Speaking of the club opening soon, I better head to the dressing room to get ready." A hollow, tense laugh popped from my throat. "You know how us girls are. It takes us a long time, but I'm pretty sure you knew that. All that primping and curling and…"

I was rambling now.

Cheeks burning, I made quick steps out the door. Just when I thought I'd made it to relative safety, a firm hand latched onto my elbow. Lucifer spun me toward him, his eyes glittering with barely controlled rage.

Uh oh. This wasn't good.

"I wasn't finished speaking with you, Sansa," he said, his lips curling back to reveal his teeth. "Isn't there something you're forgetting?"

"Um…" Panicked, I glanced at Bael and Caim. They wore matching expressions. Thin lips. Downcast eyes. Tension simmered in the room like a boiling pot of water about to spill over and burn everything in its path. "I've got to be honest with you. If there's something I'm supposed to do, I don't know what it is."

Not an ideal answer, I knew. Was this part of the game? A test? Would Sansa, the werewolf, have known the answer? Was I supposed to show my claws right now?

His smile widened. "Can't you tell what it is I want from you?"

I mean, we all knew he wanted Mia McNally to be his hellish bride, but I couldn't say that out loud. There was something else I was missing.

He curled a finger against my cheek. "I told you that you're beautiful. Your body, your hair, those eyes. I would like to take you out on a date."

My jaw literally dropped.

Wait a minute. *What?!*

Now this...this I had not been expecting. The shock of it all made me speechless for a few moments. Lucifer was asking me out on an actual date? For...dinner or something?

"This is...unexpected," I finally said in a choked voice.

That definitely wasn't the answer he wanted to hear. The smile fell off his lips, replaced by a deep, twisted frown. His eyes went dark, and the grip on my elbow tightened. *Ouch.*

"Are you telling me that you don't sense the desire between us?" he asked in a low hiss. "And here I thought werewolves were attuned to that kind of thing."

I threw a wild, desperate glance at the demons around the table. *Save me*, I shouted silently at them. But there was nothing they could do. Not without giving up on all of this.

"Yeah, I just..." I forced a smile that definitely resembled a grimace. "Well, I never thought you'd ask. You seem so...busy doing important things."

I fisted my hands when that smug smile returned. It took all my self-control not to slam said fists into his teeth. "Good. That's the right answer, darling. It's a date."

Darling. Blech.

He slammed his palm against my butt so hard it sent me tumbling down the hallway. After I caught myself, I glared over my shoulder to find he'd closed the meeting room door behind him. For a moment, I stood there, unsure, under the fluorescent light. Was he going to confront the Legion about Phenex's trap? Should I do something?

What the hell could I even do?

Tell Az.

Squaring my shoulders, I roamed through the club until I found Az near the DJ booth, checking all the dials and knobs. He shot me a lazy smile that melted my core. But now was not the time to get distracted by those kinds of thoughts. He needed to know what was happening. Stat.

In a rush of words, I filled him in. His expression grew dark when I told him about the Legion's plan. And then I mentioned that Lucifer had returned only a short while ago, unruffled and unbothered. Phenex and Valac had yet to show their faces. Not a good sign after what they'd tried to do.

"Oh, and there's one more thing you need to know." I braced myself for his reaction. "Lucifer is taking me on a date."

Shadows pulsed from within him and writhed around both of our bodies. Tendrils of smoke brushed against my skin with an electric intensity. I sucked in a breath as his expression darkened. In a dangerous growl, he whispered, "Absolutely not."

"What's the problem, Asmodeus?" Lucifer appeared from the deep shadows along the wall, his hands laced behind his back.

Az sucked in a sharp breath and pulled the shadows back into his skin. The sudden vortex left me reeling.

"My problem is," Az said in a low growl, "I haven't forgotten what happened the last time you 'dated' one of my dancers."

My brows winged upward. Ooh, this was juicy. I glanced between them, wondering which dancer he could mean. "What happened?"

"Nothing," Lucifer said with a tense edge to his voice. "Asmodeus, you have no right to interfere. Don't make me do something both of us will regret."

14

"**S**ansa," Az said, turning my way. "Do you want to go on a date with the King of Hell?"

Um, no. Obviously not. But I didn't think I had any say in the matter. Lucifer had made it more than clear that he was the one in control here, and I was just his little puppet on a string. Maybe we could find a way to turn his instruments against him, but now was not that time.

We needed a carefully constructed plan.

Az wanted me to say no. That much was clear. But surely he could see that I couldn't.

I shifted in my boots, the stage creaking beneath me. The colorful strobe lights had begun to cast pink and yellow hues on the dance floor. Soon, the doors would open. We probably shouldn't be standing in the middle of a DJ booth arguing about demon dates when the crowd poured in.

JENNA WOLFHART

"I think I need to go get ready." Gingerly, I stepped back. "I haven't done my hair and makeup yet."

"You don't need any makeup." Lucifer grinned. My god, he had the most punchable face I'd ever seen.

"Okay, thank you. Off I go." Twisting on my heels, I made my escape. I'd done what I needed to do. Now Az knew everything. It was up to him what happened next.

"Sansa," Az called after me. "You didn't answer my question."

With a frustrated sigh, I paused and glanced over my shoulder. "What question?"

"Do you want to go on a date with him?"

Frowning, I searched his eyes. They were vacant and hard, as if the fiery, electric Az I knew had vanished. There was no *zing* between us now. The demon stood before me, cold and calculating. And he demanded a response to a question I didn't dare answer.

Not truthfully, at least.

Why wasn't he letting this go?

"Yes," I said slowly, furrowing my brow. "Of course."

If I said no, Lucifer would lose his ever-loving shit.

"I see." Az's eyes shuttered. "You may go now."

Shaking my head, I minced out of the club's main room and headed to the dressing room. That

146

had been a weird-ass exchange. I couldn't very well say, *'Nope, the last thing I want to do is date the King of Hell. How about we go back to your penthouse after work? I'll give you head in the shower like we did earlier today when we were on the run from him.'*

That would be jumping right out of the frying pan and into the fire. To put it mildly.

When I pushed into the dressing room, the other girls were mostly ready. Priyanka sat in front of the bank of mirrors, half-dressed and hair uncurled. She flipped a massive golden coin. Heads. Tails. Heads again. Both sides were covered in demon seals, unlike human money. I'd never seen this kind of currency before, but it was the vacancy in her eyes that caught my attention.

I trailed over to her and placed a hand on her shoulder. She jumped. "Everything okay?"

"No." She threw the coin. It slammed against the mirror, shattering it in an instant. Shards rained down on the array of makeup and hair products scattered across the table. A hush swept through the room.

I knelt beside her, searching her tear-stained face. "Pri, what's going on?"

She glanced up at me. Her dark eyes were shot through with red. I understood at once what that meant. Pri was a fae, and they could sometimes lose themselves to the ferocity inside of them. She was barely holding on to her humanity right now. One wrong move, and she'd let loose her rage.

"Run," she hissed. "All of you should run."

"No," I said firmly, squeezing her hand. "Tell us what's going on. We can't help you if you keep it to yourself."

"I was seeing someone." Her voice wobbled as several tears spilled down her cheeks. "A wolf who lived down in the Village. We'd only been out a few times, but...it felt good, you know? Anyway, it didn't last long. The fallen angels are back to their old tricks." She motioned at the glass. "I went to see him before work. He's dead. They sliced his neck. And they left that behind."

I closed my eyes and wound my arms around her as she cried. Gingerly, Piper tiptoed over to us and fished the coin out of the shattered glass. She held it up before her eyes, squinting at it. And then her mouth dropped open.

"Oh, shit. The bastards."

"What?" I asked, turning toward her. "Whose seal is that?"

I hadn't gotten a good look at it, but I'd seen enough to recognize it wasn't Az's or Lucifer's seal. There were similarities, of course. Squiggly, twisting lines within a deeply-etched circle. But I'd studied Az's ring enough to have made order out of the chaos of those lines.

"It's Morax's," Pri said hoarsely.

My stomach hollowed out. "Morax's? The demon Eisheth destroyed?"

"It's the one thing in his life that Az has never

been able to move past." Priyanka swiped the tears away. "It's a message to him. They're pissed off, probably because he's trying to convince Lucifer that they're lying, delusional, or both. Don't forget, they know the truth about everything."

An uneasy chill slithered down my spine. In all the chaos of the past few days, it had been easy to forget about the fallen angels. They'd witnessed Az and his Legion storming in to rescue both me and Serena from their wrath. And then he'd tried to make them look like fools. We thought it had worked. Clearly not. We'd only made it worse.

"I'm sorry, Pri." Sighing, I pulled her close and wished I could do something to numb her hurt. But I couldn't imagine how she felt, especially since she'd been the one to find him lying in a pool of his own blood. "You should go home and get some rest."

"I can't," she growled in a voice that sounded far more feral than human. "Lucifer came by earlier and ordered all of us to dance, whether we want to or not. It's a big night, he said. A special guest will be arriving."

"A special guest?" I frowned. "Who?"

"It's the last person you're going to want to see," Piper said as she dropped the coin onto the table. "Eisheth is coming to *Infernal*."

*E*isheth? Gritting my teeth, I slashed my eyes with a dark liner. I needed to get out of this. And soon. Eisheth *more* than knew who I was. She'd been at that damn ball when Az had pretended he wanted to sacrifice my soul. Somehow, he'd convinced her. And *she'd* convinced Lucifer...kind of. If she saw me here now, dancing in that damn birdcage, it wouldn't take her long to figure out that she'd been had.

"I need a wig," I muttered at my face in the mirror. My features were pretty plain, at least compared to the rest of the girls. In the dark, pulsing light of the club, my eyes and nose might not stand out to a vampire like Eisheth. It was this damn blazing hair that was the problem.

I'd tried to dye it a few times over the years, of course. Just to try something a little different. The color never stuck. Within twenty-four hours, the red took over like an encroaching storm of kudzu. Nothing could battle the flames.

Ramona drifted over. She was the only girl who changed her appearance on a daily basis. Some days, she wore a short blue bob and a teensy slip of a dress that matched. Other times, she went with a more voluptuous option—long, flowing blonde hair with a red lip. Tonight, she wore something in between the two. She was a brunette with bangs, a golden gown, and a muted, natural lip. Stunning.

"I can help with that, hun. You know I love my

wigs," she said with an easy smile. "Unless you want to do something more drastic."

"What, like, run? And hope for the best?" I shook my head. "No, this is part of his game, and he wants to see my next move. He knows Eisheth met Mia McNally. He's bringing her here on purpose."

She laughed, a sound that was deep and melodic. "No, hun. I meant we could give you a glamor. Sometimes I get a little bored with my wigs and like to change things up more permanently. I must warn you, though, my powers aren't as strong as River's. Her glamors listen to her and go away when she asks. Whatever I give you…you'll stay like that for years."

"Oh." I ran my fingers through my long strands. As loud as my hair was, I didn't want to part with it. "Not tonight."

She nodded and dragged me over to her station. The table hid beneath a hundred different products, wigs, makeup brushes, and magazines. Photographs lined the mirror—the smiling faces of the girls, clearly taken across the span of several years.

"Sit." She pushed me into the chair and stood behind me, eyeing me up in our reflections. "We need to make you look as different as possible without Lucifer finding it strange. Ah, I've got it. Girls!"

Ramona clapped her hands, and everyone gathered around, even Pri. She'd rallied when she'd realized that we had a plot to pull off. Not just to save me, but everyone else that was a part of Az's Legion. If I went down, they were going down with me.

"I'm putting Mia into a wig so that Eisheth won't recognize her." She pressed her thin lips together. "But Lucifer *will* notice. That's why we're *all* going to wear my wigs tonight. If all of us decide to 'dress up' then there's nothing he can say about it. But it's just this one time!"

The girls clapped their hands and started digging through Ramona's wigs. Rolling her eyes, she got to work on my hair, choosing a bright silvery blonde.

"They're going to destroy every single one of my precious children," she said fondly.

I smiled as the girls bickered over a particularly bright pink wig. If they were going all out, then they wanted the loudest color they could find.

When Ramona finished working her magic, she stepped back and let out a low whistle. "Damn. I am *good*."

My stomach dropped as I caught sight of myself in the mirror. She was right. Ramona was incredibly good at what she did. I didn't even recognize myself, and I'd seen my face every single day for my entire life. The blonde locks flowed around a pixie face made rounder by carefully applied highlighter and bronzer. She'd swept deep purple powder around my eyes, which made them look more blue than green. My lips were fuller. My cheekbones were higher.

Goodbye, Mia McNally. Hello, Sansa.

"What do you think?" she asked, tapping her makeup brush against the table. "You've been quiet for like five minutes now. Don't tell me you hate it."

"It's perfect." I grinned up at her. "You're amazing. Has anyone ever told you that?"

"Every single goddamn day." But she lifted her chin a little, clearly touched by the compliment. "See. I don't need to use glamor to make a girl feel good."

"Right." I pushed up from the chair and wobbled in my heels. Mia McNally liked to wear boots. Sansa didn't. "Let's go put on one hell of a show."

❀

The club was already hopping by the time we made it out onto the floor. Raucous cheers went up when the cages lowered and we all climbed inside. I didn't dare scan the crowd. Eisheth would be out there somewhere. And Lucifer. I needed to stay as calm and collected as possible.

The metal groaned beneath me as I hurtled up toward the ceiling. I clung on to the golden bars to hold myself steady, wondering how I would pull this off in heels. These things swayed at the best of times, and knocking my head again would be a great way to bring unnecessary attention onto myself.

The birdcage slowed to a stop and swung on its chain. Music blared from the speakers, hectic and upbeat. I tried to calm my racing heart and give in to the feel of the music. The melody pulsed into my ears, driving out my panic and fear. And so I moved.

As the songs ticked by, I finally worked up the nerve to let my eyes wander through the club. There, in the back left corner, Phenex and Valac stood with arms crossed over their chests. Relief came like a sigh. They were okay. Lucifer hadn't gotten to them. Whatever had happened on that bridge, they'd both left unscathed.

I cast my gaze around. Stolas stood in the back right, alone. He looked as solid and unyielding as stone. Caim was down near the front. Bael stood near the door leading backstage, and Az was...

Sitting with Eisheth in a booth.

She leaned in close to him with a smug smile and tapped her red-tipped fingernail against his cheek. He responded with a grin of his own. I stopped dancing as a jealous rage whipped through me like a storm. My mouth dropped open. Blood curdled in my veins.

What the fuck was he doing? Az *hated* Eisheth.

She'd destroyed one of his Legion, and now he was tucked into a dark booth with her?

"Hello, Sansa," a voice murmured into my ear.

Shock punched me in the gut as I whirled from side to side. Lucifer had followed me up here, but where was he? Nowhere to be seen. Fisting my hands, I searched the club for any sign of him. He was doing that weird-ass thing I'd sworn Az had done when we'd first met—speak to me from a distance. *It must be a demon thing.* Eerie and creepy as hell.

"You won't find me up there, darling," he said in a purr. "Tell me, what do you think about your dear Asmodeus getting cozy with his former lover?"

I snorted. "I don't know why he's doing it, but there'll be a reason. I know what Eisheth did to him."

"You mean the death of poor Morax?" Lucifer asked. Gritting my teeth, I continued to search the club for his face. I still hadn't spotted him. Where the hell was he? "Interesting that he would share such intimate details with a wolf. He won't even discuss it with me. His *King.*"

I bit back my next retort, too close to saying something I'd regret. He was baiting me, trying to catch me off guard. It was close to working, but I was smarter than that. He'd have to work a lot harder if he wanted to see me crack.

I turned my back on the disembodied voice.

"I'm supposed to be dancing. You're distracting me."

AKA: *go away, asshole.*

A breath whispered in my ear. "Of course, darling. But I'll see you in the darkness when you're done."

15

My shift ended an hour later. Thankfully, I hadn't endured any more surprise visits from Lucifer's disembodied voice. Asmodeus and Eisheth had both vanished by the time the cages lowered to the ground. I tried not to panic about what that might mean. Az had seemed angry about my date with Lucifer, but surely that didn't mean he'd go off with his mortal enemy.

No, there would be an explanation. This was all just part of Lucifer's stupid game.

He probably wanted to turn us against each other. Asshole.

But despite my determination not to read too much into things, unease twisted in my belly by the time I got changed back into regular clothes. Az never showed as the club shut down. No one knew where he was, and Valac and Priyanka were eager to head home for the night. We waited around for a little while but locked the doors when the clock hit four.

Lucifer blocked my path when I stepped out onto the sidewalk, just behind Priyanka. He towered over me, his body pulsing with energy and rage. I swallowed hard and stepped back. I hated when he just popped up out of nowhere like this. After the whole disembodied voice thing, I'd hoped he'd leave me alone until tomorrow.

I should have known better.

"Has anyone ever told you that you're really fucking creepy?" I scowled as I tried to step around him. He shuffled left to block my way. "You're going to give me a heart attack one of these days."

"Wolves don't have heart attacks." A smile twisted his lips, and a strand of silver hair fell into his impenetrable eyes.

I sighed and folded my arms. "It's an expression. One you might understand if you made any attempt at being normal."

"Being normal is underrated." He shot closer, moving with the speed of a lion on the hunt. "I never told you the plans for our date."

"Oh. Great. I can't wait to hear where we're going." I didn't even attempt to hide the disdain in my voice.

"Tomorrow night, I'll collect you from your new home at Valac's." He fingered a strand of my hair, loose around my shoulders now that the wig was gone. "Leave your hair like this. I like the red."

My heart throbbed beneath my ribs. This obviously wasn't a genuine compliment. It was laced with a threat. He knew exactly why we'd all worn wigs, and he was angry about it. I'd made a move on the chessboard he hadn't seen coming. Good.

"Maybe I'll dye it," I said with a smile.

He stepped closer and sneered. "Best not, little wolf."

And with that, he was gone. *Thank god.*

When we reached Valac's apartment, I said goodnight and padded into the bedroom I called home. For now. Sighing, I changed into a pair of sweatpants and a *Saved by the Bell* t-shirt I'd picked up from a thrift shop the day before. The bed called to me—it was warm, soft, and safe. My entire body ached, like it had been whipped through a blender for the past several days.

Hendrix waddled in after me, cocking his head. I smiled and patted the pillow next to me. He jumped up beside me and settled in for the night.

I climbed beneath the covers and let sleep call me away.

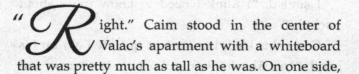

"*R*ight." Caim stood in the center of Valac's apartment with a whiteboard that was pretty much as tall as he was. On one side, he'd taped a map of Manhattan. Three street corners were highlighted by bright red circles. He held what looked like a costume shop wand in his left hand and a beer in the other. The entire Legion was here, plus Priyanka and Ramona, who both lived at Valac's along with me.

Caim smacked the wand against the map. "Rafael is back in town. So is Michael. And they're making their presence known."

A low growl rumbled from Phenex's throat as he punched his fist against his palm. "Let me have at them. I'll handle it."

Stolas cut him a dark glare. "The way you handled Lucifer? You and Valac barely made it out of that little scheme of yours in one piece."

Turned out, Lucifer had used their own trick against them. He'd found some clothes that belonged to a girl Phenex was involved with, and then he'd waved her scent all around Lower Manhattan. Phenex had been off like a rocket. If Valac hadn't caught up to him in time, Lucifer would have gotten his claws into my favorite redheaded demon.

"That was a dirty-ass trick," Phenex muttered, still punching his palm. "Using Lucinda against me like that."

I smiled. "I think I need to know more about Lucinda."

Caim chuckled, but Phenex quickly held up his hand. "No. Absolutely not. Lucinda is a terror, and

I don't want to say anything more about her.
Ever."

"I thought you had a thing for her," Ramona
said, cocking her head. Today, she wore a curly
purple wig.

"You thought wrong."

Shrugging, Caim turned back to the map. "Anyway, now that we've covered Phenex's obsession—"

"I am not obsessed."

"—we should get back to the task at hand. The
fallen angels are targeting supernaturals close to us
again." The twinkle in his eye died. "Innocents.
And they're trying to make a point."

Stolas flipped the golden coin. Morax's seal
flickered as the coin rushed up to the ceiling and
then fell like a lead weight into his open palm. I
swallowed hard. Morax had been a brother to all
five of them. Not by blood, but by something more.
A chosen family, bound by love and trust. And he'd
been stolen from them. Now the fallen angels were
using that loss to rub salt into a very open wound.

And every single one of these demons looked
ready to rip those angels apart.

"Where the hell is Az?" Bael broke the heavy
silence and strode to the door to peer out of the
peephole. "He should have been here ages ago,
lads."

"Has anyone seen him since last night when he
was with, um...?" I hated asking it. Acknowledging
his 'meeting' with Eisheth made me feel like I was

being paranoid and jealous, and obviously, I was neither of those two. *Ahem.* First, I had no reason to be jealous. We weren't in a relationship. It was just lust. Sure, he wanted to protect me, but Az wanted to protect everyone.

The only actual relationship we'd shared had been fake.

"Eisheth?" Phenex jerked up his head and shot me a lazy smile. "Someone seems a little bothered, eh?"

I rolled my eyes. "I'm not bothered. Do I need to ask you about Lucinda again?"

"Anyone who says they're not bothered is usually bothered, love," Bael drawled.

"Whatever. Don't you think it's a little weird?" I asked, folding my arms. "The last time anyone saw him, he was with his mortal enemy. The one who..." I pressed my lips together.

It suddenly felt like all the air had been sucked out of the room. Tension pounded against my skull as Phenex slowly stood. Anger rippled off his body like a heatwave. Striding toward Caim, he fisted his hands and then punched the map.

Yep, that's right. He punched the whiteboard. It toppled to the stone floor and cracked clean in half.

Caim's mouth dropped open. "Now why did you have to go and do that?"

"I was angry," he muttered. "I needed to punch something."

"Maybe a wall next time?" Caim said, throwing up his hands. "You messed up my map."

"I think not," Valac murmured from the back corner. He'd watched most of this entire meeting silently, arms draped over his knee. "If Phenex wants to punch a wall, he can go home and add to his collection of holes."

"Better I punch your wall than your face," Phenex shot back.

"Boys." Priyanka sighed and padded between them, shaking her head. "This meeting is giving me a headache. Can we *please* focus on tracking down the angels before they kill anyone else? We need to make a plan. Not do...whatever this is."

"I'm ashamed to admit this is often how we make our plans," Stolas said from his spot on the hard sofa. "They're like little children, bickering all the time."

Caim pointed at Stolas and laughed. "That's pretty rich, coming from you. Don't think we've forgotten about the time you and Bael got so annoyed with each other that you were throwing books at each other's heads. You practically destroyed an entire library."

My brow shot up. Man, I wished I had some popcorn.

"And here I thought you two were the more level-headed ones of the bunch," I couldn't help but say.

Priyanka whirled toward me and snorted. "Mia,

not a single one of these demons is level-headed. Maybe we should come up with the goddamn plan ourselves."

"Sure," I said, hopping off my stool. "You grab the marker. I'll snag the map. We can make the plan in your room and lock the door so they can't interrupt us with their squabbling. Ramona, you should come along as well."

The demons jumped to their feet and held up their hands. Objections peppered the air. Bael and Stolas grabbed one end of the whiteboard each and hauled it back to its feet. Valac was the only one who didn't move. He stayed on his spot in the corner, watching with piercing eyes.

"We'll behave, okay?" Caim said insistently when I tried to swipe the map from the broken whiteboard. He danced away when Pri lunged for the marker. "They're using Morax against us. Don't block us out of this, Mia. That's not fair."

My heart squeezed at the look on his face, and I retreated. "Fine."

Priyanka and I retook our seats, exchanging knowing smiles with Ramona. We'd actually managed to shut them the hell up. Hopefully, it would last long enough to make this plan.

Unfortunately, we didn't come up with much. Time flew by as we brainstormed ideas, and the sun slowly set outside the floor-to-ceiling windows. Orange hues splashed onto the stone, transforming the floor into burning embers. As the sky darkened, a full moon glow joined the sky. The day was gone, and all we had was a flimsy, half-baked plan.

"We'll take to the streets tonight," Phenex said firmly. "Our only option is to go on the hunt. Lucifer will be distracted by Mia. Should give us enough time to rip out their hearts if we find them."

What did it say about me that the most bothersome thing about this conversation was the Lucifer bit? I was getting too comfortable with the whole heart rippy thing.

"Well, I'm glad this torturous date will be a positive development for you," I said with a laugh.

Inside, my whole body felt like it wanted to shrivel up and die. The brighter the moon grew, the closer I got to my date with the King of Hell. I'd thought about feigning sickness but soon realized that wouldn't work. Wolves don't really get sick like humans do. I couldn't even have some sort of fake accident. My job wasn't an excuse. I had no family nearby. None of the excuses I'd conjured would work.

So the date would go on. At least it meant I could help the Legion.

If I couldn't go with them to rip a supernatural serial killer's heart out, at least I could do the next best thing: fake date a demon. Hey, I was a pro at that by now.

16

The knock on the door was the sound of my death knell. Or maybe I was just being dramatic. As I wrung my hands by my sides, Valac vanished from the living room, leaving me to face my cruel fate alone. Coward.

Priyanka had leant me a casual pink dress for the evening after I opted out of purchasing something specifically for a date with a demon king. I refused to do anything Lucifer would consider actual effort. It might make him angry, but I wouldn't give him the satisfaction.

Steeling myself, I opened the door. Lucifer stood on the threshold in a fitted black suit. His silver hair hung past his ears, matching the gleam in his eye. The essence of death pulsed around him, dark and electric. His gaze swept across me, and he smiled. Disgust roiled through me.

"Darling, you look exquisite," he purred.

I really didn't like this darling thing.

"Thanks. You look okay, too." Actually, he looked terrifying, even in the suit. How did he walk down the city streets without freaking out every human he passed? He was impossibly tall and brimming with pure horror. Couldn't they see that he was *clearly* an immortal being who wanted to consume their souls?

Of course, it was New York. There were a lot of strange sights in this city. Maybe they thought he was a *Witcher* fan doing a demented cosplay. I could believe that if I didn't know the truth about him.

He was a wolf, blending in with the sheep.

And I was one of the fucking sheep.

"Come along." He held out an arm and winked. I didn't take it. "I know a lovely little place you'll enjoy."

I rolled my eyes but went along. There wasn't anything else I could do at this point.

That 'lovely little place' turned out to be the Waverley Inn. The very place Az had taken me on one of our fake dates. Lars, the vampire mob boss, had seen us there together. He'd come over to the table to get a sniff of me and wax poetic about how good I must taste.

It was *exactly* as creepy as it sounds.

And now this whole thing made a little more sense. This wasn't a date. It was a trap. Lucifer was dragging me in front of every supernatural who had met Mia McNally, hoping to catch me out. It was all part of his stupid infernal game.

I slowed as we approached the restaurant doors to give myself time to think. This was a supernatural haunt, and Az had mentioned Lars liked to come here. If the vampire saw me, I was in big trouble.

"Is something wrong?" Lucifer stepped in front of me to block my view of the patrons through the windows. "You're looking a little pale, Sansa."

"I've been here before." I grabbed the first words that popped into my mind. "Quite a few times. The food isn't great. Maybe we could go somewhere else."

"Really? How strange. Because I have also been here. Quite a few times. And the food is excellent."

He took my elbow and gripped it tight, steering me toward the door. How gentlemanly. Much to the shock of no one, it turned out that Lucifer was pretty much the opposite of a good date. We were going to eat in this damn restaurant, whether I liked it or not.

Wonderful.

He practically shoved me inside. I stumbled in my boots. The brunette hostess at the podium let out a little gasp of surprise and dropped a stack of menus on the floor. She blushed furiously, kneeling to gather them back into her arms.

"Apologies." She shot a nervous glance up at Lucifer's face. "Your Highness."

Your Highness. My eyes rolled all the way out of my head.

She jumped to her feet and dropped the messy stack of menus on her podium. "Come with me. Your table is ready for you."

She led us toward the dimly lit back corner while speakers pumped out folksy music...or that was where I thought she was going to take us. Instead, she found a table right in the center of the restaurant, surrounded on all sides by fully packed booths and tables.

Lucifer motioned for me to sit.

So this was his play. He was going to parade me in front of everyone to make sure I wasn't missed.

If it wasn't so annoying, I'd call him smart.

After we were seated, I held the menu up to my face. I tried to cast a few subtle glances at the other booths to see if I could spot anyone who might recognize me. So far, so good.

"Tell me, Sansa." Lucifer shoved the menu aside. His eyes sparked with anger as he leaned forward. "What's your favorite dish on the menu?"

"Don't you mean *least* favorite?" I snapped back. "Because I'm pretty sure I told you I'm not a fan of the food here."

He laughed and leaned back in his chair. "How rude. At least lower your voice so the servers can't hear you."

"I don't think they care. They're not the ones cooking it."

"You really are a feisty one, aren't you?" He cocked his head, revealing the edges of the swirling tattoo along his neck. "Has anyone else ever told you that before?"

Unease slithered through me like a venomous snake. Someone had in fact called me feisty before. Not too long ago, actually. It had been Lars.

Heart hammering, I forced myself to keep my gaze forward instead of looking around. That was what he wanted me to do—search the restaurant for the vampire mob boss who'd invited me to that damn Covenant Ball.

"You sound disappointed." I arched a brow. "Not enjoying the date? Feel free to bail if you're not having a good time. I'll happily go elsewhere for dinner."

"You're playing a dangerous game, little wolf," he growled.

I stared at him for a long moment, tension throbbing in my veins. He knew I was Mia McNally. And he knew that I knew he knew. A part of me wished he'd just get it over with and say it out loud. Put me out of my misery. End this right here and now. But I knew what would come next if he did. He'd hand me a one-way ticket to Hell.

I leaned back in my chair and smiled. "So are you."

I expected him to laugh at me or maybe even growl. Anything but what he actually did. A flash of what looked like fear went through his eyes. The smug smile vanished. He looked almost...confused.

"What's going on inside that pretty little head?" he murmured.

I wrinkled my nose. "I think you know exactly what is going on. None of these dishes sound appealing. I'd like to go somewhere else."

Just as quickly as the confusion appeared, it vanished again. "You have terrible taste."

"Clearly. If I'm on a date with you."

That strange expression flickered across his face again, and he set down his menu. "You're not what I expected."

"Good." I picked up my menu, but my mind made no sense of the words. I was too distracted by what he'd said.

You're not what I expected.

All this time, Az and I thought Lucifer was somehow responsible for whatever had happened to me. Human or not, I had a weird scent and missing memories. It all seemed linked to the King of Hell. *He'd* tracked down the contract. *He'd* killed that old man. He seemed to know way more about me than I did.

And yet, he made it sound like we'd never met before.

"What did you expect?" I asked, my voice sounding far more strained than I'd intended.

"Someone a little more soft."

I jerked up my head. "Soft?"

172

"Oh yes." He gave me a smile full of teeth. "The way you were raised doesn't exactly inspire strength and ferocity."

I set down the menu, wondering where the hell the servers had gone. If I was going to get through this night, I needed a drink. Maybe five of them. Promptly.

"I'd say the opposite is true. Growing up as a werewolf isn't exactly easy."

"Hmm." He flagged down a server as she passed. Nervously, she pressed her palms against the black cloth tied around her waist. And then she took our orders. I just asked for a salad. I couldn't stomach anything more than that.

I took the opportunity to glance around. No sign of Lars or any of his vampire friends. It seemed impossible that he wouldn't appear right at the worst moment imaginable. Lucifer had brought me here for a reason, and it wasn't because he liked the food.

The first hour passed without any drama. I had a glass of wine. And then two. My starter came, one I absolutely did not order. It was a plate of shrimp with their eyeballs still attached.

I did not eat it.

I was on my third glass of wine when I started to relax. The warming buzz of the alcohol swirled through my stomach, and there hadn't been a single sighting of creepy vampires. That was, of course, when things got weird.

Lucifer stood and dragged his chair over to my side of the table. He smiled as he settled down beside me and draped his arm along the back of my chair.

I furrowed my brows. "Um, what the hell are you doing?"

"It's a date, Sansa." He pushed my hair behind my shoulder and leaned in. *Sniff.* "Typically, dates share some physical affection."

I whole-body cringed. With a shaky breath, I shifted a little further away from him. "I didn't get the sense this was that kind of date."

"Why wouldn't it be, Sansa?" he murmured against my ear. "Is there someone else in your life? Are you not single?"

"Just because I'm single doesn't mean I want to jump into bed with the King of Hell."

"I'm not telling you to jump into bed with me." He dragged his nose along my neck, just below my ear. "I'm telling you to give me a little kiss. Nothing more."

Telling me. Not asking. God, this guy was a dick beyond the whole evil demon overlord thing.

"I don't kiss on the first date," I said stiffly.

"I said I want a kiss." His voice filled with darkness. "It was not a request."

Nodding, I pushed up from the chair. "Yep, I think I've had enough. Here's a hint. Next time you want to date someone, don't order her to kiss you."

He gripped the back of my neck and yanked me down. My butt hit the chair so hard my teeth clattered together. Leaning closer, he growled. "I don't think I've been clear. I gave you a command. You obey it. If you don't, I will find the thing you love the most, and I will destroy it. And we both know what that is."

My heart pounded my ribs. The thing I love the most. *My sister.*

Tears burned my eyes, and I quickly blinked them back. I couldn't let Lucifer see that he'd gotten under my skin. Anger quickly rushed in to replace the fear. He'd threatened my sister. That was one step too far, even for the King of Hell.

"You're really going to make me do this?" I asked with a bitter laugh. "Don't you think it's a bit pathetic? Having to force a girl to kiss you by making threats?"

"It *would* be pathetic," he said, his lips curling, "if I actually had any inkling of desire for you. But you're just a little toy. One I'm having a great deal of fun playing with."

He grabbed my face and yanked me toward him. His lips crashed into mine. I screwed up my face and tried to pull back, but I was trapped there. The scent of ash filled my head.

"I can't believe it," a familiar voice growled from somewhere outside my field of vision. It was the melted chocolate tone of Az.

With a grunt, I yanked out of Lucifer's grip and

jumped to my feet. But Az was already out the door. My heart slowed to a stop.

Lucifer stared up at me with a smug smile, waiting for my next move.

Realization crashed over me. So *this* was what he'd planned. It had nothing to do with Lars and the vampires. He'd wanted Az to walk in on us kissing. So he could see Az's reaction. And then mine. I was Sansa, not Mia. I shouldn't care what Az saw.

Checkmate.

"You're a monster," I hissed at him.

And then I ran.

17

Fuck Lucifer. Fuck his game. I would not play it anymore. To Hell with it.

I threw open the door and stormed onto the sidewalk, my blazing hair a tornado around my head. Az was halfway down the block, striding forward with his hands tucked into his pockets. A cry of alarm got stuck in my throat like a rough boulder. There he was.

I cleared my throat. "Az!"

He stiffened. His hands fisted by his sides, and his steps didn't slow.

Heart twisting, I jogged after him. "Az, wait. You have to hear me out. I know this sounds cliche, but that *literally* wasn't what it looked like."

He finally stopped and twisted toward me. Pain flickered in his eyes, so harsh and raw that it sliced through me like a knife. "I know what I saw. I thought he wouldn't be able to get into your head the way he has, but I was wrong."

I stepped toward him, crinkling my brow. "Get into my head? Trust me. That's the *furthest* thing from the truth."

His gaze swept across me. "You're saying he hasn't been suggestive to you?"

"Suggestive?" I shrugged. "Sure. He's suggested that if I don't do what he wants, he'll rip apart everything I know and love. With lots and lots of violence."

The pain in his eyes vanished, replaced by the flames of vicious anger. His hands fisted, and when he spoke, his voice was low and dangerous. "He threatened you?"

"Very much so. Why else would I have gone on a date with him? It definitely wasn't because I want to spend any kind of time with him."

He sighed. "I should have known. And the kiss?"

I pressed my lips together. "He forced it."

Venomous anger bounced off his skin, transforming into swirling shadows. He strode toward me with a determined set to his jaw. When he finally reached me, he swept me up into his arms. I was crushed against his muscular chest. Relief loosened the tight grip that stress had on my body. I leaned against him, breathing him in. The fiery scent was so strong, I swore smoke filled my head.

"I see we've given up." Lucifer strode up behind

us with his arms clasped behind his back. "Time to wave your little white flag of defeat?"

Az pushed me behind him, squaring off against his King. The two demons glared at each other in the middle of the busy sidewalk while I held on to the back of Az's shirt. I didn't really like hiding, but...Az was the demon, not me.

"Sansa is mine. I'm claiming her."

Lucifer laughed. "Of course you do. You must have a new thing for redheads. I hear Mia has quite the mane herself."

"What can I say," Az said flatly. "I like fire."

Lucifer leaned sideways and gave me a little wave. "Darling, why didn't you tell me you have feelings for our dear Asmodeus? Why agree to go on a date with me? Were you trying to make him jealous?"

"You didn't give me much of a choice," I muttered.

"True." His smile dropped. "It's odd, isn't it?"

"What's odd?" Az growled.

"Has no one else noticed the sky tonight?" He folded his arms as he tipped back his head to stare up at the clouds.

I shifted on my feet. This felt like another one of his little traps. Probably a good idea to ignore him. Following his gaze would give him exactly what he wanted. But my curiosity couldn't contain itself. What was in the sky? Rolling my eyes at own damn self, I looked up.

The sky was black. Beneath the glow of the city, it was impossible to see any stars. The only visible light in the sky was the—

Realization slammed into me. I stumbled back, my hand pressed to my lips. The only light in the sky was the full moon.

Sansa was supposed to be a werewolf.

I should not be out tonight. Not in this form, anyway.

Now *this*. This was the real checkmate.

Az pressed his back against me. Shadows whorled around us, hiding us within the darkness of his demonic energy. Several humans stumbled to a stop to gape, but Lucifer didn't look at all fazed. If anything, an evil, eager glint was in his eyes. We'd walked right into his elaborate trap. Not one, but two snags to trip us up. And we'd fallen over both of them.

How had we not seen this coming?

"Mia McNally." Lucifer rose his voice to be heard over the roar of Az's pulsing shadows. "I have waited a very long time to finally meet you. Such a tricky creature and in such a strange form."

"I don't know what any of that means," I shouted back.

Heart thundering in my chest, I gripped Az's arms. He kept his back against me as we slowly edged down the sidewalk, away from Lucifer.

"You are so unlike what I expected," he called back, still smiling.

"Az, what's he talking about?" I hissed. "Why has he waited a long time to meet me?"

"I don't know, Mia," he murmured. "But we have to get you out of here before he gets his hands on you. I won't let him take you to Hell."

"He doesn't seem very concerned that we're walking away from him."

"No." Az shook his head. "He doesn't."

Az slowed to a stop. So I did, too. Whatever he did, I would shadow him. Not that I didn't think I could protect myself...I mean, who was I kidding? As much as I prided myself on being strong as hell, what exactly could I do to stop Lucifer from whisking me away to Hell?

I needed magic. Or something. And I didn't have it.

"Hold on to my shoulders." The urgency in Az's voice sent a tremor down my spine. I peered around him to spy Lucifer conversing with none other than Lars and his vampire buddies, who had appeared at precisely the worst moment. Just like I'd expected. He was gesturing in our direction. Excitement flickered across the vampires' faces.

I had a pretty good idea what was about to happen. Lucifer was siccing some vampires on us. Great.

"Az," I warned, turning back toward him.

His powerful black wings shot from his back, nearly slamming into my face. Fear throttled my heart. Before I could talk myself out of it, I wrapped my arms around his shoulders and clung on to his neck. He pushed off the ground without a warning, and a cry ripped from my throat.

Gasps and screams peppered the air as he soared away from the streets. There was no telling how many humans had seen us, and I didn't even care. We were breaking supernatural laws, but how could that matter when we were already on the run from the King of Hell?

Lucifer didn't follow us. When I craned my head over my shoulder to catch sight of him down below, I found him watching us with detached curiosity. Arms folded, head cocked. The vampires were shouting and punching their fists in the air, but Lucifer looked completely unfazed.

The game was over. We'd lost. Why was he letting us escape?

18

The Legion was waiting for us when we returned to Valac's apartment. They all sat around the broken whiteboard, surly and annoyed. So much for their fallen angel hunt. If their scheme had succeeded, they'd be blasting music and clinking beers.

"What's going on?" I glanced around the silent room.

"Ask him." Phenex nodded toward Az, sighing. "He called the whole thing off before we even had a chance to threaten a single asshole into giving us information."

"I can't believe we wasted Mia's date," Bael muttered. "We could have gotten these arseholes while Lucifer was preoccupied."

"How was the date, anyway?" Caim asked, lifting his brow. "You're back earlier than I thought you'd be."

My lips flattened. "It wasn't exactly a successful date."

"Uh oh." Phenex folded his arms and leaned back in his chair. "What'd he do? Force you to drink some blood or something?"

Az and I exchanged a heavy glance. I didn't know how to tell them how badly we'd failed. Their futures had depended on my ability to play the game, and I'd fucked it up by chasing after Az. Hell, I'd fucked it by going on the date in the first place.

The King knew that Az's Legion had turned against him. He would not let this betrayal go unpunished.

"Did anyone happen to notice it's a full moon?" I asked in a small voice.

Stolas furrowed his brows and glanced out the window. His lips parted. "Oh, fuck."

"Oh fuck is right," I said. "We all thought he would try to trip me up on the date—and he did—but the real test was whether I'd even go. Since I'm not a werewolf, I didn't even think about the damn moon. It never even occurred to me. And Serena has been so busy with work lately that I haven't spoken to her all day."

"Dammit." Phenex jumped to his feet and stormed over to the nearest wall. He hauled back his fist and slammed it clean through the paint.

Valac loosed a very long and very weary sigh from his ever-present spot in the corner. "You will be paying for that."

Phenex whirled toward him, vicious anger in his eyes. "I won't be paying for a damn thing, Valac. Don't you get it? This won't be our home for much longer. Lucifer is going to force us back to Hell and sentence us to decades of torture. Your pretty little walls don't matter anymore."

My heart skipped a beat. "Torture?"

"Oh, yeah." Phenex huffed. "You think he'll just let this go? He will remind of us who we are and what our purpose is. And he will do whatever it takes to strip our fondness for humanity away from us. He'll make us return to our base forms, and I don't know about the rest of you, but the demon I once was horrifies me."

Tears bubbled up in my eyes. Phenex's words rocked me. Their fate had been in my hands, and what had I done? Knees buckling, I slid to the ground. My words came out a whisper. "I am so sorry."

"Mia." Caim was by my side in an instant. He wrapped his powerful arms around me and pulled me against his chest. "This is not your fault. You can't blame yourself."

"Isn't it?" I peered up at him through blurry eyes. "I had one job. Keep Lucifer occupied. Play my role as Sansa, the wolf."

"We all missed the full moon. Priyanka and Ramona did, too," he said gently. "We've been a part of the supernatural world a lot longer than you have, and if anyone should have spotted it, it should have been us. Not you."

I shook my head and pulled back. "I still would have messed it up. Something else happened..."

I couldn't bear to say the rest, so Az told the story. When he got to the part about flying away, everyone groaned. Even Valac.

"So we're fucked," Phenex said. "Well and truly fucked."

"Not quite," Az said with a calmness that defied logic. "Isn't anyone curious where I've been all day?"

I perked up a little at that. His absence had been strongly felt at the meeting, despite how easily the others had tried to shrug it off. I might be the newest member of the crew, but I knew it wasn't normal for Az to miss something as important as a serial killer hunting session. He'd been determined to take down the culprit for well over a year.

And after that coin they'd left behind...it was personal.

"Mia here was convinced you were with Eisheth," Caim said with a smile that didn't quite reach his eyes. He was still rocked by the news we'd failed. I didn't blame him.

He folded his arms. "I was."

Heart pounding, I stared at him. He almost looked smug. Not what I would have expected from him after our reunion in the streets. If he'd spent all day with her, did that mean he'd stayed the night? My gut twisted just thinking about it.

I couldn't stand the idea of another woman in Az's bed, let alone *Eisheth*.

Everyone turned to stare at me. Fisting my hands, I shifted on my feet.

"Well, this should be good," Phenex muttered.

"As you all know, Eisheth worships Lucifer," Az said smoothly, like he hadn't just dropped the bomb he'd spent all day with his murderous ex-girlfriend. "He brought her into the club last night to trip us up, knowing that Eisheth's met Mia." He shot me a smile. "Smart idea, that wig. But I made sure to keep her occupied so she wouldn't pay close attention to any of the dancers. Just in case. She's more clever than she looks."

"All right," I said slowly, my eyes pinned. That still didn't explain why he'd felt the need to spend hours by her side.

"Turns out, Lucifer has been confiding in her about his plans." Az leaned back on his heels. "I managed to coax a little information out of her, but it took time. Hence why I was gone all day."

"Coax?" My voice hitched.

"Calm down, love," Bael said smoothly. "Our Az would never touch Eisheth with a ten-foot pole. He would have just been *suggestive* with her. He's done it before, trying to get the details about Morax's resting place out of her."

"One day, it will work," Stolas said with a nod.

187

"That information is in her head. We just have to find it."

I whipped my head toward Az. "You mean you used your weird demon magic? I thought it didn't work on supernaturals."

"It doesn't. Most of the time." Az let out a heavy sigh. "That's why it took so long. I had to shower her with drinks and compliments. And I had to call in another favor from the fae, just to get some magic in her head. She finally caved and told me everything."

"So you didn't..." I cleared my throat.

"Use his dick to convince her?" Caim laughed.

I flushed and glanced away. "Yeah, fine. I admit it. That's what I'm asking, okay? Now, can you all please stop staring at me like that?"

"I would never, Mia," Az said in a steady voice.

Heart thumping, I nodded. Now that we'd gotten the embarrassing stuff out of the way, it was time to focus on something else. Please. For the love of god.

"So what did you find out?" Caim asked, jumping off his stool to tend to the broken whiteboard. He popped the cap off his dry erase marker and got ready to write.

"Two things," Az said, pacing the floor. "First, Lucifer is protecting an asset uptown. A demon who knows the truth about Mia."

"Wait, what?" I glanced at the Legion, all six of

them. "But I thought you were the only demons in Manhattan."

"We're the only Princes," Stolas corrected. "But there are plenty of regular demons running around. Unlike most fae and werewolves, they tend to be a little reclusive, particularly during the day."

I gaped at Stolas. There were more of them. Were these 'regular' demons anything like these guys? Or were they worse? When I'd first met Az, I'd wondered if he had a tail or was hiding big glowing red horns. I'd been relieved when I found out neither of those things was true.

But maybe these other demons were exactly like that.

And one of them had answers about me.

"What's the second thing?" Valac murmured from the back corner.

"She knows where Rafael and Michael are hiding out. I've got us an address."

The room went so silent I could have heard a pin drop, even without a demon's enhanced hearing. Even Caim had nothing to say. Phenex managed to avoid punching another wall. After a long, tortuous moment, Valac was the one to speak.

He pushed up off his stool and strode into the light. "Neither of those two things save us, Az. We've been found out. It's all over now. We're done."

"You're right," Az replied, his voice growing hard. "Lucifer has finally confirmed the truth about

JENNA WOLFHART

us. Our fate is inevitable. But as of now, we are still standing on this earth, and we can not give up until the flames of Hell surround us."

"What are you saying?" I whispered to him, strangely touched by the intensity of his words.

"We came to this world for one reason only." He scanned the room, meeting the gaze of every demon who stood before him. "This might be our last chance to protect the lives of this city, human and supernatural alike." And then he turned to me. His eyes pierced the very depths of my soul. "This demon knows the truth about Mia, and Lucifer has been hiding him. Maybe he knows something that can save her from this fate. Maybe there's a way she can stay here."

My stomach dropped to my toes. Sucking in a sharp breath, I crossed the room and grabbed his arms. I searched his face, desperate for some sign that what he said was wrong. He acted as though there wasn't any hope for the Legion. He seemed convinced their fate was sealed.

Well, I wouldn't accept that.

"There's got to be something else we can do," I insisted. "What if we left the country?"

He shook his head. "Lucifer will find us wherever we go."

"Well, then we fight him, like you planned to do before," I said, throwing back my shoulders. "You and the Legion were dead set on destroying him only a few days ago. What's changed now? Let's come up with a plan, surround him, and do the whole rip out the heart thing."

His jaw clenched as he gazed down at me. "You're right. We have to try. But first, we'll take care of this."

I opened my mouth to argue with him, but he wouldn't hear it. He'd made up his mind. Quickly, the demons scrawled out a plan. The Legion would split up. Phenex, Caim, Bael, Valac, and Stolas would take down the fallen angels. Az and I would go alone to track down Lucifer's hidden asset—the demon with all the answers.

And we were leaving now. There wasn't any time to stick around and find out if Lucifer would pop by, armed to the teeth.

Just before we stepped out the door, Az grabbed my elbow and drew me to his side. The way he looked at me made my knees wobble. That, plus the adrenaline rush from what we were about to do, made my entire body feel like it had been tossed through a blender.

"I need you to promise me something, Mia," he said in a rough voice that invited absolutely zero argument. Whatever he was about to say wasn't a question, but a command.

"Let's hear it." I tipped back my head to meet his gaze.

"We don't know exactly what we're walking into tonight," he murmured. "I've heard about this demon. She's stronger than she looks, and she operates on a short fuse. Do whatever I tell you to do and stay close to me."

"Sure." I palmed his chest, wishing that I could take back the past several hours. I'd notice the moon and call off the date. Tomorrow would be another normal day. Or at least as normal as it got working at a demon club. Lucifer would still be playing his game, but at least I'd have more time with Az.

At any moment, he could be ripped away from me. Or I could be ripped away from Az. Because even if we both ended up in Hell after all this, I knew Lucifer would never let us come face-to-face. Not for a very, very long time.

"Az," I said, my heart pounding. "I'm not ready to say goodbye to you yet."

"I'm not either, Mia." He cupped my face. "I've only just found you."

That weird *zing* made another appearance, but for once, I didn't care what it meant. Nothing else seemed to matter right now but Az. He leaned down and brushed his lips against mine, lighting up every inch of my skin. Closing my eyes, I pressed up onto my toes and let my hunger loose. Our mouths crashed together; our bodies became one.

I needed more.

Desire burned through me.

"Ahem." Phenex coughed from the open doorway. "Sorry to interrupt, but...now is not the time to rip each other's clothes off, guys."

Cheeks burning, I unwound myself from Az's body. Phenex was right, as much as I hated to admit it. The sooner we got out of this apartment, the better.

Because Lucifer would come for us. Eventually. And we couldn't be here when he did.

19

The uptown address ended up being *way* uptown, past the point I'd ever travelled during my four short months in the city. Inwood felt more like an entirely separate borough rather than the northern tip of the island. A different kind of energy pulsed against my skin as we strode down the quiet streets.

It was calm and peaceful. Children were playing in a nearby park, and the shorter buildings provided an unobstructed view of the sky. We came to a stop outside of a red-brick building that stretched across most of the block. A sidewalk tunnelled between two matching sections, leading to a door with a pristine green awning. It looked like something on a postcard.

The normality of it all caused my skin to prickle. By this point, I would have been more relaxed about something visibly creepy. Like an abandoned warehouse or a basement apartment.

The safer it felt, the more wrong it seemed.

"You sure a demon who worships Lucifer lives here?" I whispered as we strode toward the revolving door. "This looks like a place for very human humans with Netflix subscriptions, screaming babies, and dishwashers."

Az cracked a smile, despite the potential danger that loomed before us. "Dishwashers?"

"Well, yes. Doesn't this look like the kind of building that has dishwashers in the apartments?"

"I can't say I've ever thought much about the characteristics of dishwasher apartments."

I rolled my eyes. "Of course you haven't. I bet you've had access to dishwashers your entire life. Those of us without piles of money don't always get them."

"There are no dishwashers in Hell, Mia," he murmured.

"Oh." Right. Good point. And now he was hours—or moments—away from being dragged back to that place. I had no idea what to imagine when it came to Hell. I'd asked Az to describe it to me a few times, but his expression always darkened and he walked away. Memories of that life clearly haunted him. None of the demons wanted to go back. The only thing I knew was there was a lot of fire there.

And zero dishwashers.

We stopped outside the door, and Az jammed his thumb against every single buzzer. There were about fifty of them in total. At least a dozen irritated voices blasted through the tinny speaker.

Who is this?

What do you want?

You just woke up my baby!

Finally, the door *buzzed* as an unsuspecting fool let us in without confirming we belonged here. Az and I minced inside. Well, *I* minced. Az strolled along with his hands slung into his pockets, unbothered and calm. My heart was practically beating a hole in my chest, and I had to rub my palms against my jeans repeatedly.

"We should have brought the others," I whispered as the overhead fluorescent bulb flickered like something straight out of a horror movie.

"I'm the strongest," he said firmly. "And they're doing the more dangerous deed. They need the numbers going up against two fallen angels."

He was right. But I would have felt a little better with some backup like Phenex. All he'd have to do was punch a wall, and he'd get someone talking. Together, he and Az would terrify anyone.

At the end of the hallway, we found some stairs. No elevator in sight. As we climbed up to the fourth floor, I huffed out a breath.

"Maybe I was wrong," I said, our footsteps echoing against the concrete steps. "If they're making the top floor walk up six flights of stairs, they aren't putting dishwashers in all the units. Very tricky of them, you know. I bet they rent more units by making the outside look a lot nicer than the inside. Sure, you'd find out when you viewed the place, but I still bet it makes a difference."

"Mia," Az murmured with a smile.

"What?"

"Calm down. I won't let anything happen to you." He stopped me in the middle of the fifth flight of stairs and pushed me back against the rough wall. An unexpected gasp popped out of my mouth. He leaned in close, dragging his lips against my neck. A blast of heat burned through me, momentarily drowning out the fear.

"Nothing will happen to you," he growled out, his eyes flashing. "Whatever we're about to face, they'd have to kill me first before I'd ever let them get to you. And I'm pretty fucking hard to kill."

"But that's what I'm afraid of," I whispered back. "I know you'll protect me, Az. But I don't want you to lose you in the process."

His lips twisted into a wicked smile. "You have no idea what I'm capable of, Mia. And I'm not sure I want you to see it."

My heart pounded, and I swallowed hard. "If it means you survive, then I absolutely do want to see it."

I wouldn't lie and pretend I didn't feel the teensiest bit of fear. Not *of* him. I knew he'd never harm me. I could see the truth of it in his eyes. But I also knew that he'd held back. He'd kept the worst of his demonic side hidden from me. And he'd told me himself that he'd done terrible things. Most of that had been in his past, but not all of it.

He curled a finger against my cheek and searched my eyes. I knew he could scent my fear and unease, but maybe he could also smell the wild desperation. If he had to go a bit demony inside this apartment to protect us both, then so be it.

"You might not like what you see," he said. "You might never look at me this way again."

I reached up and tangled my hands in his hair. "Az. I want you to do whatever it takes."

With a nod, he brushed his lips against mine. And then we were off, charging up the rest of the stairs. We reached the sixth floor and pressed out into the carpeted hallway. It stank a bit, like old socks and cat piss.

Appearances can certainly be deceiving. The outside had given off the aura of a well-kept, peaceful apartment building. But the interior was a mess. The lights flickered. Stains splattered the walls. The ragged carpet needed to be replaced at least ten years ago.

"Definitely no dishwashers," I muttered.

When we reached the right door, Az gave me one last glance before giving it a light knock. As we waited, adrenaline surged through my veins, making me feel like my skin was going to bounce right off my bones. I'd never been more on edge in my life, and that was saying something. This was nothing compared to stage fright or the nerves before a big speech in class.

It was the unknown of it all. Neither one of us had any idea what was on the other side of that door.

The hinges creaked as the sagging door swung open. A face peered out at us, wrinkled and small. I cocked my head as I stared at the little old lady who stood before us. She was stooped over, like an invisible weight squatted on her shoulders. Her gold-rimmed glasses matched her necklace, and coils of white frizzed around her heart-shaped face.

Um...

This was the demon?

"I'm sorry." Az stepped back, confusion in his voice. "We must have the wrong address. Apologies for disturbing you so late at night."

Her rattling voice whispered out at us. "Who were you looking for, son?"

Son. I bit back a smile. If she only knew Asmodeus was centuries older than she was.

"A woman named..." Az glanced down at the paper in his hands. "Rebecca Reynolds."

"I'm Rebecca Reynolds," the old woman said.

Oh. Hmm. This was getting stranger by the moment. A little slice of fear shimmied its way into my heart as Az tried to make sense of it all. Eisheth had been the one to give him the name and address. She'd been on Lucifer's side since the beginning.

My heart began to pound harder in my chest. Was this another one of his tricks? Could we have walked straight into *another* trap?

Az turned to me. "This is the wrong Rebecca Reynolds. Eisheth must have gotten the addresses mixed up somehow."

"You know Eisheth?" the old woman asked.

Az's eyes sharpened on her face. All the blood inside my veins stilled. "Forgive my confusion, but...I must ask. Do you know what Eisheth is?"

"Oh, yes." Rebecca bobbed her head. "Vampire. Quite vicious when she wants to be."

Shadows rippled across Az's arms as he stepped forward. "But you are..."

"Human?" The old woman smiled, and for the first time since she'd opened the door, something about her face looked off. Like the lines of her nose didn't match. My stomach twisted with unease. "I'm not human, Asmodeus, and I know why you're here. You want the thing Lucifer asked me to hide for him."

Nerves jangled my belly. Rebecca wasn't human, so then what was she?

Az stormed forward and slammed his hand against the door. It rattled on its hinges, and it shot wide open to reveal a hoarder's den. The entire surface of the floor hid beneath towers of junk. Glittering trinkets. Mounds of clothes with the tags still attached. Tattered books and a random assortment of electronics. The walls were covered in framed photos. Floor to ceiling. Wall to wall. There wasn't even an inch of space left untouched.

And the thing we wanted was somewhere in the midst of all this. No wonder Lucifer had wanted to hide it here.

"You're welcome to take a look," she said with a sweet smile, motioning toward the disaster.

I didn't really know what to say at this point. What other choice did we have?

Az gave a nod and stepped inside. I followed him. Rebecca closed the door behind us and darted through the mess as if she'd done it a thousand times before. When she reached an arched door-frame leading into the kitchen, she paused where she precariously perched on a teetering pile of card-board boxes with the dexterity and balance of an Olympic gymnast.

Definitely not human.

"Would either of you like a cup of coffee or tea?"

"No, thanks," Az grumbled.

Her watery blue eyes turned toward me. "And you, dear?"

Coffee was the last thing I wanted right now, but it would be good to get rid of her for a few moments. At this point, we had a bit more informa-tion, but it wasn't much. There was an object we needed to find that somehow held all the answers. Lucifer had gone to a lot of trouble to hide it from us, and we would never find it without knowing what it was.

"Sure," I said. "Cream and sugar."

Might as well drown the taste of the brown water as much as possible. Not that I had *any* intention of consuming anything that came out of that kitchen. I refused to go down in the fourth quarter from some poisonous coffee. I'd made that mistake once. Never touch something an enemy supernatural tries to offer you.

Or you might end up bound and gagged in the middle of a demon seal, ready for sacrifice.

After she'd bustled into her kitchen, I whirled to Az and hissed my words. "What the hell do we do now?"

"We find the thing," he said gruffly.

I folded my arms. "And what is the thing?"

His lips flattened as he gazed around at the mess. "Something in this room."

"Yep. You're right. That's very helpful." I twisted toward the sound of boiling water, frowning. "What do you think she is?"

"She's what Eisheth said she is," he murmured back. "A demon. She's been hidden by a scent and appearance glamor. It's likely how she's been able to collect all this stuff. No one looks twice at an old woman hobbling around."

"Do you think she's powerful?" I couldn't help but ask.

"I think she is far more deadly than she looks, but I also think she has no plans to fight us unless we get too close to the object she's hiding."

"So we just need to poke around until she gets angry."

Az's lips twisted, his expression darkening. "Are you sure you meant what you said outside?"

"About you doing your worst?" My heart pounded. "You know I did...why?"

"It would take weeks to sort through all this stuff, and she knows it." Az reached behind his back and withdrew a sword that I had not seen until now. He'd kept it hidden, doused in his shadows. I swallowed hard. I remembered that sword. He'd named it Abaddon, and apparently, it had a mind of its own.

"Step back, Mia," he warned in a low growl. The sword flickered in response.

"Yep. Got it." I dove behind the sofa just as Rebecca Reynolds bustled out of her kitchen with two steaming mugs of coffee. A part of me felt guilty. She reminded me of my grandmother. Her sweet little face. That watery smile. The way she held the mugs as if they were a struggle.

"Oh, I see. This is how we're going to play." She cackled and threw the mugs at my face.

20

I yelped and ducked behind the sofa. The mugs shattered on the wall behind my head, breaking several photo frames. Gasping, I threw my arms over my head to protect my face from the shards that rained down on top of me. A few slivers of glass sliced through my shirt, and a stinging pain tore through my skin.

Meanwhile, I could hear Az locked in a brutal battle with the grandma demon. I popped up my head to find his sword ringing when it slammed into hers. She held a big, monstrous thing lined in jagged edges. Like a serrated knife. The hilt was black with a pair of gleaming red eyes.

And I swore those eyes were looking right at me.

"Give up!" Az roared. "Yield!"

The demon cackled once more and threw all her weight behind her sword. It arced toward his gut, and the sharp tip of it sliced through his black shirt. Az stilled, his eyes flashing with rage.

I wet my lips. Now while I appreciated his swordplay, I had to admit this wasn't the terrifying, destructive force I'd conjured in my head. My imagination had gotten a little carried away, it turned out. He couldn't rip her apart with his mind or shatter her bones with a single touch. If he wasn't currently locked in a dangerous sword battle, I might have laughed out loud at myself.

"I've had enough," Az spat, releasing his sword.

Abaddon clattered against a stack of porcelain plates. My mind screamed as I watched in horror. *What the hell is he doing?!* He couldn't just drop the damn sword. Heart shaking, I pushed up from behind the couch to rush to his aid. She'd destroy him like this. She had a massive sword and enough strength to shove it right into his gut.

Az held his hands out on either side of him and threw back his head. He opened his mouth, letting out a terrible, all-consuming roar. His shadows shot from his skin, a great massive swarm of them. I slowed to a stop, jaw dropping.

Rebecca let out a little squeal and turned to run, but the shadows consumed her before she could get anywhere. They flew into her mouth, a swarm of darkness so thick it looked like billowing smoke. Her head dropped back, and she stilled, frozen in place by the shadows.

They still pulsed around her, weaving in and out

of her open mouth and nose. Horror twisting through me, all I could do was stare.

Az strode toward her with vengeance in his eyes. "Tell me where the item is."

With a mouthful of shadows, Rebecca couldn't speak.

He grabbed her arm and whipped her toward the mess. "Show me."

Her eyes as wide as saucers, she shook her head. "Uh uh. Lmmiceffeer."

"Lucifer," Az repeated. "You're afraid he'll destroy you if you show me where it is."

She nodded.

"Unfortunately for him, I got here first," Az growled. "Show me where it is or I'll destroy you before he even has a chance to get his hands on you."

The demon trembled beneath Az. The shadows swarmed her. Every now and then, one would dart out like a knife and slice her arm. Shuddering, she dropped to her knees before Az.

She bowed her head low to the ground.

The shadows misted. The terror on his face cleared. With a heavy breath, I sat hard on the sofa, not daring to say a word. That had been intense. And as good as I knew Az could be, there was no doubt in mind he would have used his shadows to rip her to shreds if she had not surrendered to him.

Rebecca choked out the last remnants of the smoke and slowly reached toward a small black box just out of her reach. It was sandwiched between a pile of empty bottles and a stack of wooden squares. Az snatched it before her fingers could reach it.

Az held it up before his eyes. "What is it?"

"It's the thing you want," she whispered. "And now Lucifer will come here and destroy me, just like he destroyed the demon who had it before me. The one who signed the contract."

My eyes widened. So that was who the old man had been?

A deep frown pulled down the corners of Az's lips. "What does it do?"

"It restores memories."

I gasped. Az twisted toward me, his awed realization matching mine. No wonder Lucifer had tried to hide this from us. If my memories had been erased, this object was the one thing that could bring them back. This was better than a random contract outlining exactly what had happened to me.

I would be able to *see* the truth of my past.

My mouth went dry as our gazes locked. This was it then. No backing out now. With the little black box, I had to face my fears. I had to find out the truth about what I was. All of it. As bad as it might be.

"You need to leave," Az said, pocketing the box. "Drop the glamor. Get a new scent if you think you need it. Head to another city, like Vegas. In a few months' time, Lucifer will have forgotten all about you."

Rebecca's eerie laugh crawled up my spine and dug into my bones. It certainly didn't match her old lady appearance, that was for sure. "Lucifer never forgets anything. He will make me pay for this one day, Asmodeus. You should put me out of my misery before I drown in his flames of torture."

I shuddered.

The motion caught her attention. She gave me a grimace of a smile. "You don't know what you've just done to yourself, girlie. You're going to regret this."

"How would you feel if you had no idea who you were or what your past was?" I pushed up from the couch, calling upon a courage I wasn't sure I had. "And what if you knew the truth could change everything? Wouldn't you try to find out?"

She shook her head. "I just don't think you're going to like what you see."

Without another word, Rebecca leapt out of her open window. A cry of alarm hurtled from my throat, and I dodged the piles of crap to reach the ledge. Wings flared against a night sky, vanishing into the dark. I pulled back and turned to Az. He regarded me with a pained expression.

"You think she's right," I said.

"I think you need to prepare yourself for what we're about to see. Whatever it is, it's big. Are you ready?"

"Not really," I said in a small voice. "But I have no other choice. I need to know the truth."

❦

*A*z and I didn't stick around the demon's apartment any longer than necessary. We'd use the little black box to unlock my memories, but not there. We needed somewhere quieter. Somewhere more familiar. Somewhere I felt comfortable and relaxed and safe.

We ended up back at his penthouse, even though we both knew Lucifer might come by there, eventually. There was no better place to go for something like this.

While I paced in front of the couch, Az did his little security check routine at each wall. I tried to psyche myself up for what was about to happen. There were forgotten memories inside my head. The box would unlock them and tell me things I knew would shake me. When Az finally joined me, he looked troubled.

"Has he been here?" I asked.

If I were Lucifer, this apartment would have been one of the first places I would look. Of course...I probably wouldn't have watched my enemy fly off into the sunset either. But he was the King of Hell. Our logic didn't really operate in the same realm.

"No." He scowled. "I don't like it. He should

have checked here by now. It's what I would have done."

"I think we've established that he's kind of a psychopath. So what *we* would do is probably not what he would do."

"No." Rubbing his stubbled jaw, he shook his head. "He's biding his time for something, and I don't like it. What if he wanted us to find this black box?"

"You think it doesn't do what Rebecca said it does?" I flipped the box in my hands. It was fairly nondescript, and it certainly didn't look magical. "I guess I wouldn't put it past either of them."

Az held out a hand. "Let me try it on myself first."

I snatched back my hand and clutched the box to my chest. "I'm the one with the missing memories."

"Yes, but I'm..." He grabbed my fingers and slowly pried them away from the box. "The immortal demon. If it hurts me, I'll heal."

Sighing, I rolled my eyes and released my tentative grip. "Fine. But if it doesn't do anything to you, then I get to try it."

"And here I thought you were avoiding this whole thing. You didn't seem thrilled back at the demon's apartment."

"I'm not thrilled," I admitted. "And I'm scared. But I can recognize this as something that needs to be done. Maybe it will unlock some magic in me, as crazy as that sounds. And then I might have a chance of standing up to Lucifer."

Az held the box up to his eyes and squinted. I knew what he was looking for. A symbol, a demon seal. Something to give an indication of whether or not this thing had been doused in some kind of destructive spell. I'd already had a close look, though, and there was nothing there.

He bounced the box in his palm. "I'm going to hold it up to my forehead and see what happens."

With a deep breath, he lifted the square object up toward his head. For a moment, he held it frozen about an inch away from his skin. Tension pounded against my skull as my heartbeat picked up speed. I didn't want him to do this. The problem was mine, not his. But I knew he'd never listen.

Az pressed the box against his skull. His eyes rolled back into his head, and he fell.

"Az!"

I fell with him, my knees buckling. Somehow I manage to catch his head just before it slammed against the hard floor. Gently, I cradled him in my lap, pressing the dark hair out of his closed eyes.

"What's happening?" I whispered to him, tears leaking onto my cheeks. "What did it do to you?"

I glared at the tiny object that had tumbled out of his open palm. It sat just beside his left knee, still and calm, like it hadn't just knocked out a Prince of Hell. Or...worse? My fingers found the pulse in his neck. His heart still beat. He was alive. For now.

His voice echoed in my ears. *A demon cannot die. The only way to stop one is to rip out his heart and bury it away from the body.*

Okay, so that probably meant he'd recover from this. Whatever it was. If there was a spell out there that could end a demon's life, he would have known about it. It wouldn't just surface now.

Plus, I was pretty sure Lucifer didn't want us dead. If we were dead, we wouldn't suffer.

"What do I do, Az?" I pleaded with him.

My eyes cut to the box again. The best thing I could do was leave it there untouched. Find a way to rejuvenate Az and then toss the thing out of the penthouse window. Maybe it would shatter into a million pieces when it finally made contact with the ground.

But then I would never know.

Something inside me felt drawn to the box. A little voice whispered that I should use it, despite what had happened to Az. It wouldn't hurt me. Somehow, I knew I would be fine. The feeling was so clear and certain that it could have only been put there by magic.

Muttering curses at myself, I snatched up the box and pressed it against my forehead before logic talked me out of it. The box seared my skin like a hair straightener on the hottest setting. I cried out and dropped the box, pain lancing through my head.

Suddenly, the world went black.

And then a strange light filled my mind.

I blinked, trying to make sense of it. Something felt...oddly, achingly familiar. Another time. Another place. Memories flashed through my mind all at once. They filled my head with laughter, music, and tears.

Horror and awe twisted around me like twin ribbons. I suddenly knew everything. I understood it all. I wasn't actually a fallen angel. At least, not in this life.

I was the human reincarnation of one.

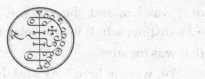

21

When I came to, Az was waiting for me. He'd lifted me from the floor and carried me over to the sofa, where he cradled me in his arms. The scent of him consumed me, bringing back those fresh, aching memories Lucifer had wiped from my mind when I'd only been a baby. I'd never signed a contract, so I still didn't understand how the old man demon had been involved. But that didn't matter right now.

"Mia," he murmured against the top of my head.

A tear slipped down my cheeks. "Az."

My heart was full of a million different emotions. The knowledge of everything I'd seen had shaken me, just as I'd expected, but this was way, way, *way* more than I'd bargained for. If Az hadn't been holding me, I would have probably run through the penthouse screaming.

"So," he said softly. "Turns out, my memories were wiped, too."

"Yeah," I whispered. "Lucifer's an asshole."

We sat in stunned silence for a while, clinging on to each other as though we'd just spent the last three hundred years apart. Because we had. Kind of. I was her, and she was me, but I was also my own distinct self. It was a weird thing to experience, that was for sure.

"We were in love," Az said, his voice soft. "Your name was Mia, even then. A fallen angel, walking the earth, lost and lonely. We even met *here*."

In New York.

It was hard to make sense of it. In my past life, Az and I had been lovers. We'd met on a wet summer night, both drenched from the rain. He'd invited me into the warmth of his ground floor home, and we'd formed an instant connection. It hadn't mattered that I was a fallen angel, and he was a demon.

For one very happy year, we'd been inseparable.

Until Lucifer found us.

"So I don't understand something," I finally said, breaking through our troubled thoughts. I knew we were both caught up in the past, trying to relive the memories of those long-forgotten years. For me, it was overwhelming to the extreme. I had two different lives now, colliding into each other. Kind of. I didn't remember everything. Only that year I'd shared with Az. Everything else from that life was still a meaningless blur.

"You want to know why Lucifer intervened," Az murmured, tightening his grip around me. "That was the beginning of the end for me. He saw me soften, how my interest in Hell began to wane. You're the entire reason I am the way I am, Mia. Before you came into my life, I had little interest in humanity. You changed me. For the better."

My heart filled with a strange kind of hope, but there was still a shadow around it. "It wasn't really me, you know. I don't think we're exactly the same person."

Az shifted me on his lap so that he could gaze into my eyes. Heat curled through me at the adoration in them. "Yes, you are, Mia. That's how reincarnation works. You are her, and she is you. The soul is the same. Your bodies are different, but that hardly matters."

"So angels have souls?" I asked.

"Of course they do. Every living thing has a soul." He sighed against the top of my head. "This is why Lucifer wanted to steal you away to Hell. If he marries you, I can never lay claim to you again. The magic of a demon's ceremony is forever binding."

"Seems a bit drastic, don't you think?" With my mind still desperately trying to make sense of our shared past, I couldn't help but focus on Lucifer's actions. Obviously he hadn't been thrilled that his

main Prince had fallen for an angel who had softened his soul. But he'd made some absolutely
insane moves to deal with it. He'd found a way to
destroy me as permanently as possible, and then
he'd wiped Az's mind of me.

"He managed to kill me," I said, glancing up at
him. "We're supposed to be immortal. And by we, I
mean, the old me. And you."

"That's the thing, Mia," he said, fingering a lock
of my hair. "He didn't kill you. You're here."

"But my body..."

"Found a way to come back," he said with a
dimpled smile. "You fought your way back to life,
just like any other angel or demon has done when
destroyed. You pieced yourself back together, the
only way you could. Into a mortal body."

But that meant...my old heart was still out there,
beating in the dirt.

Weird.

I let out a heavy sigh and leaned into him. This
was still incredibly difficult to wrap my mind
around, even though the memories were fully
inside my head now. It was me, but *not me*. Separate
and yet together. It was going to take a long time for
me to fully come to grips with it.

"So what do we do now?" I finally asked.
"While this has been *extremely* informative, it hasn't
really solved our problem. I'm human now. I don't
have any powers. What's going to stop Lucifer from
making me his bride?"

"Hmm." His voice rumbled against my ear. "I think you might not be as helpless as you think."

I cocked my head and frowned. "What do you mean?"

He slid his finger beneath the chain around my neck, the one that held his signet ring. "Remember when you got cornered in that alley? You were able to use this without any prompting from me."

"Well, sure. Kind of." The momentary blast of power hadn't done a great deal of good, and the ring didn't always do what I asked it to do. When I used it, it liked to shut down for a good few days.

"If I handed this ring to pretty much any other human in this city and didn't tell them how it worked...nothing would ever happen."

"So you think I have powers?"

"I think there's a hint of it in your blood." He pulled me against him, sighing. "But I don't yet know how we can use that to our advantage. Have you ever done anything else you couldn't explain?"

"Nope. Before moving here, the only magic I ever had in my life was Serena." Thinking of Serena, I frowned. She had no idea that any of this was happening, and I needed to call her before it was too late. The last thing I wanted was to be stolen away from earth without having a chance to goodbye to my best and oldest friend.

Pain flickered in my heart. I did not want to leave this place.

"That's right," Az murmured. "You helped her

through her early shifts. And you were immune to her werewolf venom."

"That's right," I whispered back, my heart pounding. "I'd almost forgotten, but you're right. I was immune. And the fae magic got to my head faster than normal, didn't it?"

Tension released its grip on Az's jaw, and he finally smiled. "You have some magic in you, Mia. I don't know the extent of it yet, but it's there. And we will find a way to use it to protect you from the King of Hell."

Speak of the devil...

My cell rang. Az and I locked eyes. Somehow I knew who the caller was without even looking. Slowly, I pulled the phone out of my pocket and lifted it to my ear.

"Lucifer," I said with an edge in my voice. He'd been the one to do this to me, and a vengeful anger I'd never felt before swirled through my veins. Somehow, I would make him pay for this. For ripping me away from Az. For snuffing out my previous life. For stealing away every memory I had of our past.

He'd ruined so much. I wouldn't let him destroy anything else.

Our past was done, but at least we had our future. As long as we stopped Lucifer.

"Hello, Mia. I trust you found the little black box of memories," he said in a sickly sweet tone that dug into my skin. "How are you feeling after all your shocking revelations?"

"Pretty pissed off actually," I snapped, narrowing my eyes. "What do you want? Why are you calling?"

The one thing I didn't understand was why Lucifer had let us go that night. At that point, I still hadn't known a damn thing. Neither had Az. Had he not wanted to risk a scene in the middle of the Manhattan streets? Or was it something else? It almost felt like he'd wanted us to find that box.

Why go to the trouble of hiding my memories if he wanted me to find them, eventually?

"You and Asmodeus were never very good at games, even in your past life," he said, his voice turning as hard as steel. "Try as you might, you just don't have that natural inclination toward chess. You see, you need a strategy. The pieces need to fall into place. The Rook goes here. The Queen goes there. Done correctly, you've won before the game begins."

"Stop speaking in riddles, Lucifer."

"Eisheth doesn't enjoy being used," he hissed. "Asmodeus should know that by now. Do you really think she would spill my deepest secrets after a bottle of wine and whispers of suggestive lies?" He laughed into the phone, making me wince. "Every single step of the way, you've done everything I wanted you to do. Including this."

My heart pounded against my ribs, the phone

cracking beneath my tightening grip. "If you wanted me to remember my past life, why didn't you just hand me the fucking box to begin with?"

"Boring." I could hear the smile in his voice. "And I needed *something* to keep Asmodeus occupied tonight."

My breath stilled. I glanced over at Az. He was watching me with a pinched expression on his face. He could hear every word.

"I have your Legion, Asmodeus," Lucifer said. "And if you do not do exactly as I say, I'll destroy every last one of them."

22

We met Lucifer on the roof of Az's building. Wind whipped around us, rustling the hair around my shoulders. On the horizon, the distant glow of the sunrise peeked over the skyline. It had been a very long night. Weariness tugged at my bones. But the time for sleep was a long while away.

Lucifer had Az's Legion.

I'd never seen anything more horrifying than the look on Az's face when he'd heard those words. The heartbreak in his eyes had nearly crushed me.

Lucifer thundered to the concrete in a crouch, his wings flared wide behind him. He slowly stood, towering over the both of us, but Az didn't even flinch. Shadows of rage pulsed from his skin. Daggers shot from his eyes. He would make Lucifer pay for this.

He held his sword in one hand and my fingers in his other. We would face this one side by side.

"Well, don't you two look happily reunited?" Lucifer regarded us both with deep-seeded disdain as his wings folded into his back. "It's sickening."

"Where are they, Lucifer?" Az asked in a low growl. "What have you done with my Legion?"

"You should really start addressing me as Your Highness." He tsked, the wind tousling his silver hair. "I loosened my grip on you far too much over the years. I let you do whatever you wanted. Look at where it's gotten me."

"Where. Are. They?" Az tightened his grip on his sword and stalked toward his King, releasing his hold on my hand. And then the weirdest thing happened. I swore I heard a roar from the sword.

Lucifer arched his brows and held up his hands. "Stand down, Abaddon. If you slice off my head, you'll never find them. I'm the only one in the world who knows where they are."

The sword sizzled with heat.

Az lowered Abaddon to the ground. "You've made a massive mistake targeting my Legion. I've never been more determined to rip out your heart than I am right here, right now."

Lucifer laughed. "Based on your reaction, it's the best decision I've ever made. I have your attention now. And you'll do exactly as I say unless you want them to end up like Morax. Hidden forever."

Az's entire body began to shudder. With my

heart breaking for him, I wrapped my hand around his and pulled him back. His shadows whipped around him, desperate to attack. Lucifer had stabbed him right where it hurt, and he knew it. If only I had some actual useful magic, I would smack that smug smile right off his face.

"You've made your point," I said to him, throwing my arm out in front of Az. He was barely holding on to his anger. "Now tell us what the hell it is you want."

Lucifer's eyes bored into me. "I separated you once, and I'll do everything in my power to separate you again. It seems you won't do it willingly, so it's time I intervened. Go your separate ways, Mia. Permanently. Never see each other again. Do this, and I'll let the Legion live."

My heart slammed my ribs as I stared at him. I blinked, trying to make sense of it. That was what this was all about? All the plotting, all the scheming...it was just *this*? He didn't want us to be together. That was...all.

"So you don't want me to be your bride?" I asked slowly.

He snorted. "Marrying you meant he could never claim you. So yes. That was my first choice. Then I met you and realized being bound to you for eternity would be a nightmare."

"Fine with me," I snapped. "Feeling's mutual."

"That means no Hell for you either," Lucifer said, lifting his eyes above my head to smile at Az.

"She can go free, Asmodeus. No harm will come her way. But you must part. Permanently."

Heart hammering, I twisted toward Az. I could already see in his eyes that he was going to agree to this. He would do anything to save his Legion. And he'd do anything to save me.

I grabbed his arms and tried to catch his gaze. "We don't have to do this, Az. There has to be another way. We can *fight* this."

"I'll give you two days to make your choice." Lucifer's wings rippled behind him as he pushed up toward the sky. "Expect some instructions shortly."

23

The silence of Az's apartment pounded against my eardrums. The quiet was intentional. The walls were soundproof, and we were several dozen stories up in the clouds. Up here, the frantic hustle and bustle of New York was nothing more than a whisper.

But it made my thoughts too loud.

I curled up on the couch and watched Az pace in circles. Anger and despair rushed across his face in waves. He looked ready to throttle someone, and then he looked crushed. On and on and on it went until I couldn't stand it anymore.

"Az," I said softly. "We need to make a plan. Let's call some of the others here. They might be able to help us come up with something."

"The others?" He barked out a bitter laugh. "The others are gone, Mia. He took them from me."

227

"No." I pushed up from the sofa and stepped in front of him. He ducked around me and kept pacing the floor. "He's hidden them somewhere. Probably in Manhattan. If we put enough heads together, maybe we can come up with something. We can track them down before our time is up."

"What heads?" he asked, his voice as sharp as steel. "Valac is gone. Caim is gone. Bael is gone. Phenex is—"

I motioned toward the door as a knock echoed through the penthouse. Az furrowed his brow as I strode over to it and let our guests inside. Serena, Priyanka, Ramona, and Piper poured into the apartment with pizza, beer, and Hendrix.

Az looked dumbstruck as they set up camp in the middle of the living room. Hendrix waddled over to the kitchen to poke around, and the girls spread a subway map across the coffee table. Serena had even rustled up a whiteboard that she propped up in front of a lamp. As I settled onto the floor beside her, she gasped and buried her face in my hair.

"Mia." Her cheek pressed against mine, damp with tears. "I swear to god, if you ever run off and do something stupid without me again, I will track you down and absolutely obliterate you. I have claws. I will use them."

"I'm sorry," I whispered, pulling back. "Things have gotten a little out of hand."

"I mean..." She blinked at me. "Understatement of the century."

"Multiple centuries, it turns out."

She cocked her head. "What does that mean?"

"I'll explain later," I whispered. "Right now, we need to focus on why I called you over."

When Az and I had returned to the penthouse, I'd sent out an SOS to the girls. They'd been more than eager to help, especially when they learned of the demons' fates. We might not have the experience of the Legion when it came to mystery solving, but we had something just as important. A lot of love and determination.

We immediately got to work, poring over the map Priyanka had found at the club. The one Valac had spent all those years on, detailing every corner, every building, every room inside this crazy city.

It was...a lot.

"So." Priyanka glanced up from the section she was studying. "What are we thinking? Could he have hidden them close by?"

"It sounds like something he would do," Piper said with a nod, her blonde bob bouncing on her shoulders. "You know how much he likes to play games. It'd be like hiding them right under our noses."

"But surely that's too easy." Serena frowned. "Wouldn't he expect us to start looking in Hell's Kitchen?"

"He wouldn't expect us to look in Hell's

Kitchen," Az said with a growl, stalking over to where we'd set up shop. "Because he knows I have no choice but to acquiesce. Searching for the Legion is completely pointless. We won't find them unless Lucifer *wants* us to find them."

"Fuck Lucifer," Priyanka said with a shrug. "Maybe it's time he doesn't get what he wants."

"She has a point." I dropped my chin onto my knees and wound my arms around my legs. "Just because he tells us to jump doesn't mean we have to jump."

Az shook his head and stormed away. The door of his bedroom slammed behind him, reverberating through the silence. With a soft sigh, I stood and brushed the pizza crumbs off my jeans.

"I should go after him." I nodded toward the maps. "You three see what you can come up with."

Pri peered up at me with a sad smile. "I'd say he'll be okay, but I worry that'd just be a lie."

"I won't let it be," I said firmly, following Az's footsteps to his room. During the time that I'd known Az, he'd put so much on the line to protect me, to keep me safe. It was time I repaid the favor and did the same for him. I'd do whatever it took to get his Legion back.

I pushed the door open and closed it as quietly as I could. Az stood beside the window, curtains thrown back. He stared out into the darkness of the night. It was late enough that some of the high-rises had gone dark, but the twinkle of the city still lit up his room like stars.

"I know you're hurting right now, but I won't let you give up." I joined him by the window and dropped my head against his folded arms. "You're Asmodeus, the First Prince of Hell. If anyone can take on Lucifer, it's you."

"You really believe that. Don't you, Mia?"

"I've seen what you can do." I turned to him. "If you used those shadows against him, you could win."

He frowned. There was little hope in his expression. "Did it ever occur to you that Lucifer's powers are even worse than mine?"

My stomach flipped. "Sure, but—"

"I've failed them." His voice was pained.

The door suddenly flew open, and the thunder of footsteps followed. A tornado of muscles, sweat, and blood hurtled into the room and slammed right into Az. I stumbled back, mouth dropping when I caught sight of Caim's familiar head of long dark hair. He clutched his arms around Az, nearly choking all the life out of him.

"Caim?" Az's voice came out a whisper at first. And then he wrapped his arms around Caim's back and roared. "Caim!"

I pressed my hand to my mouth, overwhelmed by emotion. Tears poured out of my eyes, my chest shuddering. The relief I felt wobbled my knees, and I had to sit hard on the bed before I tumbled to the floor. I'd had no idea how terrified I'd been until Caim strode in with his big smile and boulder biceps.

"You're okay," I whispered, terrified to believe it. Maybe this was another trick. Lucifer could have gotten to the fae and made someone else look just like our Caim.

But no, Caim couldn't be faked. He was too much personality in that massive frame.

He pulled back from Az and held out an arm. I leapt to my feet and joined the hug, leaning into the both of them. We formed a circle, shoulder against shoulder, thigh against thigh. All the hope I'd had was suddenly magnified.

If Caim was safe, maybe we really *could* do this.

As if reading my mind, Az stepped back and dropped his fisted hands to his sides. "Where are they? Is Lucifer with them? How easily can we get them out of where he's holding them?"

Caim winced. "You're not going to like this...I have no idea. When the vamps jumped us at the warehouse, we fought like hell. Managed to take out a few of them. Phenex was on the warpath. But one of them sneaked up on me and hammered my face with a massive plank of wood. When I woke up, everyone was gone, and there was a letter left for me."

Az's jaw rippled with anger. "Where's the damn letter?"

"It's gone. Burned up as soon as I'd read it."

"Damn witches," Az cursed. "What did it say?"

"Same thing I'm guessing Lucifer told you, judging by your reaction when I walked through that door." Caim sighed. "He's taken the Legion. If you and Mia don't go your separate ways, he's going to destroy them."

Az growled.

"What's going on out there?" Caim jerked his thumb at the door. "Looks like Legion 2.0 with all the maps and beer."

"They're trying to help us find a way to get the Legion back," I said softly. "We thought we might be able to figure out where Lucifer is hiding them."

"Ah." He nodded. "I see."

"And now that you're here, you can help." I paused halfway across the floor. Az and Caim hadn't moved from their spot beside the window. "Aren't you coming? We don't have much time."

Az and Caim exchanged a weighted glance and then followed me back into the living room. We all settled into our roles, scanning the maps, looking at Valac's notes. Lucifer had visited New York on at least three dozen occasions during the past several decades. He never stayed long, so it was easy to track his assets and the buildings he owned.

After several long hours, the midday sun poured into the quiet penthouse. I could barely keep my eyes open, and the girls weren't having an easier time themselves. When I'd nodded off for at least the fifth time, Az finally gathered me in his arms and carried me into his bedroom.

"We need to keep looking," I whispered, too tired to raise my voice any louder. "We need a list of places to check..."

"You need to sleep first, Mia." He gently lowered me onto the bed and climbed in beside me. With a sigh, I curled up on his chest, giving up the fight to stay awake.

"I don't want to sleep," I whispered as my eyelids grew heavier than an elephant's feet. I'd definitely been awake for over twenty-four hours, and not a single one of them had been relaxing.

But if I slept, I'd lose the last hours I might ever spend by Az's side. I wanted to squeeze out every last drop of time we could. In my past life, I could have fought against sleep for days. No such luck now. I might have a little magic in my veins, but I was still one-hundred percent human.

"You can't keep going like this, Mia." He pressed his lips to my forehead. "At least sleep a few hours. Then you can pick back up your notepad and pen. You can scribble away your plans as long as you'd like."

"Not as long as I'd like," I pointed out. "We don't have much time."

"Sleep, Mia," he whispered.

I opened my mouth to argue. As tired as I was, I couldn't ignore that we were both in his bed. And there was no telling what would happen tomorrow.

Or...later today, actually. Maybe this bed should be used for something else other than sleeping.

I reached toward him.

But he'd done that damn thing to me again. The one that made me rest.

The shadows of the past filled my mind.

24

Terror charged through me. I sucked in a deep breath and flew up straight, damp hair plastered to my forehead. Breath heaving, I glanced around. Black silky sheets. The murmur of distant conversation. The scent of fire.

I sagged back against the bed and tried to calm my racing heart. Panic had wrapped its claws around me while I'd slept. Not entirely surprising. I'd been dreaming about our shared past, and all I could see was Lucifer's twisted smile when he'd plunged a knife into my chest.

Shaking the thoughts away, I reached across to the other side of the bed. It was cold to the touch.

Where was Az?

After throwing my legs over the side of the bed, I padded to the door and peeked into the living room. Only Az and Caim remained awake, sipping on gin and tonics topped with lime. They looked tense and angry, the lines on their faces deep and raw.

"I just keep thinking about Morax," Caim said with a shake of his head. "Losing him was the hardest thing I've ever been through."

"You know I feel the same," Az said quietly, swirling his drink. "His death ripped me apart in an unimaginable way. I never really recovered from it."

Caim glanced up. "I know, Az. We all know."

His grip tightened on his glass. "I've failed them. You, too. I should have kept you safe, but I was the one who sent you after those fucking fallen angels."

"We would have gone anyway, Az," Caim muttered. "You know we would have."

"Not if I'd told you to stand down." Sighing, Az pushed up from the chair and refilled their drinks. I wondered how many they'd had by now. Maybe I should join them. A drink might help me relax.

"It's sweet what the girls have tried to do for us," Caim said as he approached the scattered maps on the floor. He picked through them one by one and then crumpled several sheets into a ball. "Too bad it was a bunch of wasted effort. Lucifer would never let us get near the Legion, even if we found them."

"I know." Az turned toward him. His eyes were hollow and dark. "We've lost them, haven't we? Their fate is sealed. Not unless I do what needs to be done."

Caim shuddered and then took a long gulp of his drink. "I don't want you to do this. There has to be another way. If the others knew...they'd never agree to it. Surely that has to mean something."

My heart thundered, and I inched a little closer to the door. I'd thought I knew what they were talking about, but now I wasn't so sure. What was it Az planned to do? Whatever it was, it didn't sound like it matched up to what we'd been discussing all day. Find the Legion. Destroy Lucifer. Live happily after ever. *All* of them. Including Az and me.

"I have to, Caim." Az closed his eyes. "It's the only way to keep the Legion and Mia safe. I'll give myself up to Lucifer, and everyone else can go free."

Shock punched me in the gut, and I pressed a shaking hand to my heart. *No*, I mouthed, grateful no sound came out. He couldn't be serious. Az couldn't mean this. The last thing anyone wanted was for Az to sacrifice himself.

He continued. "Lucifer made it clear. He'll let everyone live if Mia and I part ways permanently. You saw the look on her face, Caim. She'd never leave my side. The loyalty I've always wanted is right here in front of me, and I have to walk away." His face screwed up in pain. "But it's what I have to do."

Caim downed his drink and slammed it on the table. "You think this is the solution, but it's not. You know what will happen, don't you? Not a single one of us will let you face Hell on your own.

239

If you go, we'll go. That's how it's always been, and that's how it'll always be."

"No," Az growled, stalking toward Caim. "You will stay here and continue on with *Infernal*. That's an order, Caim."

Caim shrugged. "I've ignored orders before. I have no problem ignoring them again. Not when it comes to this."

"Dammit, Caim!" Az shouted.

I ducked back into the room, my heart hammering. I'd heard enough. No wonder Az had been so strange during my meeting with the girls. He'd never had any intention of following along with our plan. He'd been stewing in his dark thoughts, preparing to sacrifice himself.

And Caim was right. If Az went, they would follow him, no matter how hard he fought them on this. They were a family. And family stuck together.

I blinked back a fresh wave of tears. Az was wrong. There *was* another way for us to end this. My presence in this city was the problem, and it always had been. Lucifer's words had been clear. No one had to go to Hell. Not me. Not Az. Not his Legion.

With my chest burning, I darted through his room and threw some clothes into a bag. His t-shirts mostly, and a pair of boxers. I had nothing else here with me, and I'd need a few clothes and some cash for the road. At least for a little while. Until I found my feet again.

I didn't dare stop by my Brooklyn apartment on the way. He'd think to look for me there. So would Lucifer. I had to do this right so that neither one of them could ever find me.

I wouldn't let Az submit himself to a life of torture. Not when there was another way.

After throwing the bag over my shoulder, I hovered by the door, listening for an opportunity to escape. When the demons drifted into the kitchen for another drink, I took my chance. Breath held in my throat, feet as soft as I could manage, I whispered out his bedroom, into the corridor, and out of his life forever.

25

The summer sunshine brought the crowds out to the Brooklyn Bridge. Elbows rammed into my side. Screaming children raced by. It was an unwanted cacophony of sights and sounds, but I hadn't known where else to go or what to do.

My scent was now a massive fucking problem. Az's words echoed in my mind. He'd never forget my scent. It was imprinted on his mind. And I was pretty sure that included the new werewolf glamor. As long as I stayed the same, one of them would find me.

"Well, well, well." River strode up to where I leaned against the bridge, her hands laced behind her back. Even with her neon pink hair and glittering skin, she didn't stand out on a New York day like this. "When I got the call, I could hardly believe it. Mia McNally, needing a favor? *Again?*"

I'd gotten the fae's number off Serena after making up a story about finding a lost fae in the streets. It had pained me not to tell her what I was really doing, but I couldn't risk her calling Az so they could try to stop me.

My heart felt hollow as I gave River a weak smile. There were so many goodbyes, and I hadn't had a chance to say any of them. "Turns out my life is pretty complicated."

She sized me up, nodding. "That can happen when you run with the likes of Asmodeus."

"It's not Az's fault," I said sharply. Sighing, I rolled my eyes at myself. "Sorry. I didn't mean to snap at you. It's been a rough few days."

"I heard. Lucifer cornered you at the Waverley Inn and finally got the truth out of you." She joined me along the edge of the bridge, leaning against the railing. "It's all over the news, you know. Your little flight in front of all those humans. They're trying to make sense of it. Thankfully, none of them have gotten close to the truth."

I shrugged. "I honestly couldn't care less at this point. I'm just trying to survive."

"Your red hair is a key feature." She nodded at the loose strands around my shoulders. "It's a unique shade. You won't be able to hide for long if you keep it like that."

I glanced down, frowning. My plan didn't cover the hair issue. I'd called River here to ask for another scent glamor. Nothing more. But she was right. Lucifer had said as much. My facial features might not stand out in a smaller town, but my hair would. It could end up being the very thing to lead Az—or Lucifer—straight to my door.

"So I've got to change the hair," I finally replied. "Anything else?"

"You have a cute little nose." Smiling, she had the audacity to bop it.

"Um, excuse me?" I pulled back, arching my brow. "No bopping."

She shrugged. "It's cute."

"Cute enough to identify me as me, even with the other changes?"

"Eh." She cocked her head. "Probably not."

I took a deep breath and nodded. Unease flickered in my belly, and I didn't know why I was so nervous. It was just a little glamor, nothing more. But it felt like the final, brutal nail in the coffin of my future. New York was my home, and I had to leave it. Wherever I went, I knew I'd never find another place quite like it. Maybe I'd be able to settle in somewhere and find contentment. But I'd never feel alive the way I had here.

As if the entire world had opened up before me.

Part of that was Az. His Legion. That club.

Even if I somehow made it back here one day, I'd never be able to go back to *Infernal*.

"So what it'll be then, Mia McNally?" River asked, her lilting voice cutting through my thoughts.

Sighing, I turned her way. "Scent and hair."

"What kind of scent?" she asked as she placed a warm hand on my collarbone, just as she had the last time.

"A demon might be fun," I said with a sad smile. "Or hell, even a vampire. But it would probably just get me into trouble. Let's go with human."

"Human?" She chuckled. "All right. I'm guessing you don't want it to be anything like the other one."

"Yeah, that would kind of defeat the entire purpose of hiding myself."

"I have to check..." She leaned in close and whispered into my ear. "I won't do this for free."

Heart pounding in my ribs, I nodded. "What do you want in return?"

"It doesn't work like that, Mia." Her laugh echoed in my mind. "You'll owe me one. And when I come calling, you'll have to pay up."

Wonderful. That definitely couldn't go wrong. It was like writing a blank check, only you had no way of knowing when someone would cash it. She could come for me in a year. Or maybe ten. Decades could pass before she decided to yank the chains of our deal.

"So?" she asked with a smile.

"Yeah, it's a deal. Go on and do it. It's not like I have any other choice."

She pressed her hand against my arm, and invisible flames rushed across my skin. Gritting my teeth, I swallowed down my scream, knowing that if I made a scene, I'd only bring more unwanted attention onto me. Az or Lucifer would find me before I'd even left the city.

When she was done, she stepped back and nodded. "You look better as a redhead, but the brown's not so bad."

I glanced down. My once-brilliant hair was a deep chestnut. The color I'd always envied in high school. It clashed with my pale skin, and it brought out a frizziness I'd never had before.

River saw me looking, and she shrugged. "Sorry. Sometimes color changes can fry the hair a little."

I scoffed. "But it's a glamor. It's not real."

She patted my arm. "This one's real. It'll stay like that until you wash it with rosemary."

"That's it?" I asked as she drifted away, joining the crowd bustling along the bridge.

She called over her shoulder. Her long pink hair brushed her waist. "That's it, hun. You're on your own now. Good luck."

❀

After gathering up the broken shards of my heart, I boarded a train heading north. My plan was to do the exact opposite of my first instinct. Az might expect me to head down to Tennessee. I had family there, even if they wanted nothing to do with me. My sister might find a way to sneak me some money, just enough to keep me going for a little while.

It made sense. It seemed like the safest, most logical thing to do.

So obviously, I couldn't do that.

What was up north? Snow. Cold. Mountains Not a single person I knew. That was perfect. The demons wouldn't have the foggiest clue where to look first. As long as I had no idea what my next move was, I'd be unpredictable.

I'd be like smoke.

The train rumbled along the tracks as it left the city behind. Soon, the countryside rolled by the windows. It didn't take long for the imprint of New York to vanish, the tall, towering buildings replaced by wild bushes and grass.

At some point, I dozed off, still weary from the past several days. A hand landed on my shoulder and shook me awake. Startled, a sharp cry shot from my throat, and terror tripped through my veins. I reached for something to protect myself with, but my hands found nothing but the soft bag full of Az's clothes.

"Hey, hey," a kind, soft voice said. "It's all right. I'm sorry I startled you, but we've reached the last station. Thought you might have missed your stop..."

I glanced up at the woman smiling down at me, my heart still racing. For a moment, I panicked. Did she recognize me? Had she called the cops? But then a strand of hair fell into my eyes. Brown hair. Not red.

Letting out a breath, I tried to steady myself. "Sorry. I was fast asleep and just got startled. Thanks for waking me."

"What's your stop, hun?"

I nibbled on my bottom lip and glanced out the window. There was a single platform just beside us. Beyond it, a field stretched out for miles. No sign in sight. I had no idea where the hell I was.

"This one," I said brightly, hoping I didn't look and sound as delirious as I felt. "I'll get off right here."

Concern flickered through her eyes when I turned back to her. "You sure you're all right? Do you need any help?"

For a moment, my voice got stuck in my throat. This woman seemed so earnest. The smart thing to do would be ask her for help. I'd have to lie about some of the details—I didn't think she'd believe me if I started ranting about demons and fallen angels. But the kindness in her eyes drew me in. Maybe she could help me find somewhere to stay.

No. I shut those thoughts down. It was too soon to ask for help. I didn't have a good story, and I didn't want to make it up on the fly. One bad move, and the wrong people would find me.

"Like I said, I just got startled." I gave her the most genuine smile I could muster. "I was in the middle of a weird dream and got a bit disoriented. Thanks for offering, though."

That was finally enough to get her moving. She trailed down the corridor and vanished out the door while I gathered my bag and tried to calm my racing heart. I hadn't been lying about one thing. My dreams were super weird. I kept picturing Lucifer's terrifying smile as he stabbed me over and over again.

When I got off the train, it turned out I'd landed in a rural town in Vermont. I hadn't even known I'd crossed state lines, let alone gone that far north. A sunset streaked across the skies, lighting up the world in pink and orange hues. The air was cool against my bare arms as I lumbered out of the station and into town.

It looked like something out of one of those made-for-TV movies. The main road cut through a tree-lined street full of aesthetically pleasing red-brick buildings home to crafty boutiques and artisan coffee shops. Most of the businesses were already closed, but I spotted a Bed & Breakfast at the end of the block.

I waffled a bit as I approached. I needed something more like a motel, a rundown place where no one would want to banter about the weather or ask about my family and health. These Bed & Breakfast people would be chatty. I could tell by the cute animal trinkets hanging in the window.

Unfortunately, I didn't have another choice that I

could see. With a sigh, I trudged inside and asked for a room from a bubbly teenager behind the front desk. Likely the daughter of the owners.

She showed me to my room, handed me a welcome pack, and left me alone without peppering me with a million questions. Maybe I'd misjudged the place. Or maybe she could tell I needed to crawl into bed.

I'd never been more tired in my life, and I knew this was only the beginning. I had no idea where I was going or how I'd get the money to survive.

The motto of the Legion rattled in my head.

One day at a time.

26

Ten hours of sleep did my body a lot of good, but my mind was still frazzled. It felt like I'd stuck my finger into a light socket. Repeatedly.

I'd done it. Shocking, really. Getting out of New York had happened in a whirlwind of panic and fear, and I hadn't fully thought things through. But I'd done it. Now I had to figure out my next step.

After showering and tugging one of Az's shirts over my head, I tried to ignore the overwhelming scent of him and get on with things. I'd paid for two nights at the B&B, but I needed to plot out my next move now.

A knock sounded on my door. Ah, there it was. The intrusion I'd been expecting. They'd left me to sleep all morning, but their curiosity would have gotten the better of them by now. Who was their new guest? Where had she come from? And why was she wearing a shirt that was three sizes too big?

I'd had all night and morning to plot my story. I'd lean in to my southern roots and distract them with stories about my childhood when they got too inquisitive about my current situation. There'd be no mention of New York. And definitely no talk of demons.

When I pulled open the door, my eyes were met with a dark, fitted t-shirt over sculpted muscles. My eyes followed that shirt up to a familiar throat and jaw. Despair rushed over me when I met Asmodeus's gaze. I shook my head, stepping back. How the hell had he found me?

"Mia," he said roughly, hands fisted by his sides. "What the hell are you doing here?"

"I was actually going to ask you that exact same question," I whispered.

A part of me was relieved to see him. My body yearned to rush toward him and leap into his arms. It had only been a day, and I'd missed him so much my soul hurt. But I couldn't. I'd left New York for a reason.

"Why do you think I'm here?" he asked, turmoil rolling through his eyes. "To track you down. You vanished, Mia. I've been losing my fucking mind."

I winced and craned my head around the door-frame to check the corridor. This probably wasn't the best conversation to have anywhere that there might be curious ears. "We should probably talk inside my room."

"Fine," he growled, storming inside and slamming the door behind him. I winced. "Mia, how could you have left like that? I thought Lucifer had gotten to you. I thought you might be dead."

"I figured it would be obvious," I whispered harshly as my own hands began to shake. "I overheard you talking to Caim. You were never going to try to save the Legion by fighting. You were going to sacrifice yourself and spend an eternity in Hell. And every single one of your demons would have followed you. Caim, Phenex, Bael, Valac, Stolas. You'd be trapped there. For a long, long time. Did you really think I would be okay with you doing that when there was another solution right in front of us all this time?"

All the words tumbled out of my mouth in one breathless rush. All my thoughts and feelings were twisted up together, tearing me apart from the inside out. He shouldn't have come here. We'd been so close to fixing everything. How had he even tracked me down?

"*This* isn't a solution." He gestured at his shirt, at the room, at the fact he was here. "Those are the only clothes with you. Aren't they? What about cash? Do you have any?"

I swallowed hard. "I had a little. I used it to book this room."

"How much is left?"

"Um, five or six dollars?"

"Right." He folded his arms, shadows whipping across his skin. "And what are you going to do when that runs out? Where are you going to stay? How are you going to eat?"

"Well." I folded my arms right back at him. "I was in the middle of figuring all that out when you barged into my room."

"You have no money. No clothes. No job. What about an ID?"

I didn't have any of that. There'd been no time.

"Look, I know my situation isn't exactly ideal," I finally said with a sigh. "But you know what's worse than this? You and your Legion stuck in Hell for the rest of your lives...which is pretty much forever, based on what you've told me."

He closed his eyes, his body practically humming from the intensity of his emotions. "Mia, this isn't your burden to bear."

"I love the Legion, too, Az." My words came out a choked whisper.

He flipped open his eyes, and his gaze pierced me, hot and electric. "You heard what Caim said. The Legion won't let me sacrifice myself for them. The same goes for you."

"Except Hell and a B&B are two *entirely* different things."

"You won't be in this B&B for long," he argued.

"Not unless you have a secret stash of unmarked bills that you've kept on the down low all this time."

Unfortunately, there was no secret stash. Would have been pretty helpful, though, right?

"How did you even find me?"

"Mia." He grabbed my hand and pressed it onto his heart. The rhythm of it pumped against my fingers, threaded through with that *zing* that always got me at the strangest times. "I can *feel* you, deep within my bones. I closed my eyes and called for you, and that feeling brought me here. I know it sounds crazy, like I'm out of my goddamn mind, but it's true." He closed his eyes. "Until I reached out and called for you, I thought you were dead. Do you know what that did to me? I swear to god, I—"

I clutched his chin and kissed him fiercely. A cry choked out of his throat, and his hands found my hips. I stumbled back as his body collided with mine. Both of us were frantic. Frenzied. Like the world was crashing down upon us, and our only hope was to cling on to each other for dear life.

"Never run away from me again." He lifted me from the floor and tossed me onto the bed. The headboard hit the wall, but I didn't care. I wasn't trying to hide any longer.

He climbed on top of me. Gazing up at him, I wound my arms around his neck and pulled him to my lips. Our kiss deepened, softening. My soul lit with fire as our past and present memories tangled together. I'd loved him once, and he'd loved me. Together, we had been a force to be reckoned with, and we would have battled beside each other for centuries if Lucifer hadn't torn us apart.

And somehow, I had found him again, even if I no longer truly felt like that girl.

Az pulled back and gazed into my eyes. "I thought I'd lost you again."

"I'm sorry." I palmed his cheek. "But you can't blame this all on me. You were the one who wanted to leave, Az. You were going to give yourself up to Lucifer and let him take you to Hell."

He dropped his forehead to mine. "I know. And I was wrong to think that was the right choice. I see that now."

A small smile tickled my lips. "Did I just hear Asmodeus, the First Prince, admit to being wrong about something? Maybe none of this will end up being a problem because Hell's going to freeze over."

His lips quirked. "Don't be so cocky."

"Why not?" I slid my hands along the strong curves of his shoulders. "I have the sexiest being in the entire world on top of me right now. If that's not a reason to be cocky, then I don't know what is."

"Oh, I'll show you cocky," he said with a low growl.

He stood from the bed and slowly undressed both me and him with a patience he'd never displayed until now. His body rippled as it moved, like a perfect painting come to life. When he climbed back on top of me, I was ready for him. This felt different than before. Our walls were no longer between us, and the ribbon of our connection wound from the past and into the future, tying us together now.

A golden string.

Pushing the hair back from my face, he gazed down at me with adoration in his eyes. Our limbs tangled together, our bodies becoming one. Az kissed my neck, and then travelled to my collarbone. Arching toward him, I hooked my leg around his thigh.

His lips trailed down my skin until they brushed my core. Shuddering, I widened my legs and gripped the sheets. He dragged his tongue across my folds, and the building heat inside of me threatened to explode. I was overwhelmed by desire and the strange connection between us.

I didn't know what I would do if I ever lost him again. Now that we were together, I would fight to remain by his side.

His fingers dug into my hips as his tongue took me over the edge. I crashed against him, pleasure ripping through me like a white hot comet. As I pulsed around his tongue, he grabbed my knees and pinned them on the bed.

Gazing down at my wetness, he licked my pleasure from his lips and plunged inside of me. His cock hit the back of me, and I quaked around him. With an animalistic growl, he flipped me over, lifted my ass, and then slammed into me once more.

Heart pounding, I gripped the sheets and clung on tight when he thrust deep inside me with an intensity that left me reeling. His hunger for me lit that fire inside me again, and another ache of need pulsed between my legs.

He wound his fingers around my hair and yanked back my head. Stars dotted my eyes. I'd never been more turned on in my life. Before, we'd just had sex. This was something else entirely. He was claiming me, putting his mark on me. This was fucking and making love all mixed up as one.

"Tell me you're mine," he panted, tightening his grip on my hair.

"I'm yours, Az," I whispered back.

His thrusts deepened, his cock sliding against my slick walls. I moaned as he slammed against the back of me. I wanted more. I was so close. I could barely stand another second without more of him inside of me. Tightening around him, I rocked back my hips.

Az let out a roar that shook the entire room. He came inside of me, and the tremors of his release tipped me over the edge. My climax shuddered through me, harder than the last. Ears roaring, I gripped the sheets and held on until it passed.

We both slumped against the bed, tangled

together. His heartbeat pounded against my ear when I rested my cheek on his chest.

"So," I whispered after a moment had passed. "I guess I'm going back to New York with you."

He chuckled. "You better. Or I might have to spank you."

My cheeks burned. "I wouldn't mind a little spanking."

"Mia."

I shifted my head to meet his gaze. "Yes?"

"I meant what I said. Never do something like this again."

"All right," I whispered. "I won't. I just have to ask one question."

His fingers traced soft circles along my back. "Of course you do. Go ahead."

I slid my hand up his chest and felt his heartbeat. It was steady and sure, unlike my own. Now that my focus was back on New York, the overwhelming nerves had returned. If only everything else could be as easy as this.

"What are we going to do about Lucifer?"

"Well." He sighed. "First, no one is going to Hell."

"And second?"

"I don't know what the second part is yet," he admitted.

"That is not very reassuring, you know."

"I know." He dropped a kiss on my forehead.

"We'll return to New York. We'll make a plan. And then we'll go from there."

I nodded, understanding at once what he meant. "One day at a time."

"One fight at a time."

27

"Mia." Caim swept me up into his arms, and his dark hair tickled my cheek. "You're never allowed to leave like that again. Do you hear me?"

"I'm sorry," I eked out as he crushed me against his chest. "I was just trying to do the right thing and save you from the flamey burning place."

He chuckled, a familiar sound that warmed my heart. "Well, your little stunt did one thing. It convinced Az to fight back. So maybe it was the right thing to do after all."

"From what I heard, you weren't very keen on fighting, either." Slowly, he lowered me to my feet.

He ruffled his hair. "You're right. And that's not like me. But I couldn't see the forest for the trees. Only a temporary lapse in judgement, that's all. It isn't in our blood to give up. No matter what this world throws at us, we have to keep fighting."

"One day at a time." I smiled.

He clasped my hand in his and nodded. "One fight at a time."

Serena appeared just behind him, her hand clutching her throat. She let out a little growl and threw herself at me like a feral wolf. I opened my arms as she slammed into me. Her arms clutched my neck, and her angry tears dampened my cheek.

When she pulled back, she shoved a finger into the center of my chest. "I can't believe you left without saying goodbye. After calling me about that damn fae. I thought they'd eaten you up and spit you out. You can't *do* things like that, Mia."

"I'm sorry." I took her shaking hand in mine and squeezed. "I thought you'd try to stop me."

"Damn straight I would have," she said fiercely. "I'm not going to let you run off and face the world alone. You and me, we're a team. Always. Never do this again, okay? If you need help, come to me. I know you'd do the same for me."

"You're right." I nodded. "I would."

"We're going to figure this out together." At that, she pulled me back in for another hug. I clung on tight, regretting my decision to run. I'd only been trying to do the right thing and save those close to me, but all I'd done was cause them torment and fear. For so long, I'd depended on myself and no one else. I'd had to get by on my own. But my life wasn't like that anymore. *Thank god.* This was my team. My family.

We quickly got to work when the rest of the crew drifted in with more pizza and beer. Hendrix waddled over and poked at my foot, and I could have sworn I saw an accusation in the pigeon's eyes. I'd left him, too. But that sounded crazy. To make it up to him, I gave him his own slice of pizza.

The penthouse filled with movement and noise, reminding me of the many nights I'd spent surrounded by the Legion before Lucifer had appeared in Manhattan to terrorize us all. But a heavy cloud hung over our all our heads. The lack of the demons' presence was like a black hole sucking all the light into it. They should be here with us, plotting and scheming.

Valac should be in the back corner, watching from the shadows, his clever mind twisting ideas into fully formed plans. Phenex should barge around and make jokes about feeding our enemies to the fishes. Stolas would pore over a book with a silent determination in the set of his strong shoulders. Bael would toss a ball from hand to hand and compare our tactics to players on a cricket field.

We had to get them back.

"Only Lucifer knows where the Legion is." Priyanka settled down beside me and hung her head in her hands. "We don't have time to search every building in this city, especially not without tipping him off. He'd see us coming a mile away, and that's if we even found them. Do you know how many buildings are in this damn city?"

"Approximately five gazillion," I said flatly. "Especially if you're counting the Bronx, Queens, and Brooklyn."

She shook her head. "I don't think he would have crossed the Brooklyn Bridge. He would have stayed nearby."

Something flickered in the back of my mind as Priyanka's words cut through me. She was right. Lucifer *was* the only one who knew where he'd hidden the Legion. We didn't have time to check out every lead we'd scribbled on the whiteboard. There were about thirty of them so far, all places where Lucifer had once stayed during his trips into the city. Which meant we needed to narrow it down. *Way* down.

To one lead.

Lucifer had said instructions were incoming. Had we missed something? Something extremely important.

I motioned to Caim. He trailed over from the whiteboard where he'd been scribbling what looked like nonsense for a good half hour. "Caim, do you remember everything that letter said?"

"Sure." He grinned. "I have a photographic memory. Most of the time, it's an asset. Good for remembering phone numbers." He leaned closer and whispered. "Phone numbers from women, if you know what I mean."

I rolled my eyes. "Yeah, I think we *all* get what

you mean, Caim. How did the letter end? What are we supposed to do when we've made our decision?"

"Doesn't really matter, does it?" The smile slid from his face. "We're not handing you *or* Az over to him."

"No, but he doesn't know that," I explained. "So what's his plan? Where are we supposed to make the swap? Is he coming here? Or are we supposed to go to him?"

Caim's brow winged upward. "We're supposed to meet him at the club to tell him our decision."

"*Infernal*. That's good." I nodded. "That's *our* territory, not his."

"What are you trying to say, Mia?"

"Lucifer knows Az would do anything for his Legion, and he has a pretty good idea about the bond I share with him. Otherwise, he wouldn't have gone to all this trouble to keep us apart." I glanced over at Az, who was deep in discussion with Serena. Even now, his shadows were frantic strands whipping around his arms. He wouldn't relax until all of this was over.

"Right," Caim said. "Which is why Lucifer plotted this whole abduction scheme in the first place. It was the easiest way to get Az to do what he wants."

I nodded and met his gaze. "So we make Lucifer think Az is going to do exactly that."

Realization dawned in his eyes, and he sucked in a sharp breath. "You want to set a trap for Lucifer."

"Sounds pretty insane when you say it out loud, but...yes." I lifted the map I'd been studying. "We've tried our best here, and time is running out. We'll never find where he's hiding them unless we get extremely lucky. Think that's going to happen?"

"Probably not," he muttered. "Az might not like this. I know we planned to fight Lucifer, but we wanted to find the Legion first. Otherwise, it's just me and Az up against him."

"You don't have to fight him by yourselves," I said with a meaningful arch of my brow.

"You?" Caim shot me a lopsided smile. "You know I love you, Mia, but you're human."

I wrapped my hand around the signet ring. "I still have Az's ring, and I haven't used it in weeks. If I wait for the right moment to blast it, Lucifer will never see it coming."

Caim shook his head and caught Az's attention with a flick of his fingers. As he left Serena to join us, Caim spoke out of the corner of his mouth. "Just going to warn you now. He's not going to go for this."

"Go for what?" Az folded his arms, and his swirling shadows reached toward my heart.

"Mia's had an idea." Caim grinned. "Haven't you, Mia? I'll let you fill him in on your little plan."

"Should have known you'd be a coward," I muttered.

"It was your idea," he said in a singsong voice.

I rolled my eyes and told Az about the plan. We'd pretend to go along with Lucifer's demands, get the Legion back, and then surround him. While Az and Caim distracted him with battle, I'd blast him with the ring. It would be enough to catch him off guard and give the demons a chance to...well, rip out his heart.

"I don't like it," Az growled.

"Told you," Caim said.

"It doesn't matter if you like it or not," I said, narrowing my eyes. "There aren't any other options. We have a few hours until we're supposed to give him our decision, and Lucifer will make his move regardless of whether or not we meet him to make the trade."

"I don't want you anywhere near him." His voice was firm and unyielding, but I wasn't going to back down that easily.

"It's not up to you." I squared my shoulders and met his eyes. "It's my life, and it's my decision to make."

He captured my face in his hands and searched my eyes with an intensity that made my toes curl. Even here, in front of everyone, when we were hours away from our potential deaths, I wanted him desperately.

"I know you remember a time when you were

strong and powerful and brimming with magic." He pressed his forehead against mine. "But you're human now, Mia. Your life is fragile. I can't let you put yourself in that kind of danger."

"But that is precisely why I *should* do it," I whispered back. "Lucifer will never expect me to do a damn thing. He'll be focused on you and Caim. I am not a threat to him."

He shook his head. "I don't like it."

"And I don't like the idea of you sacrificing yourself to Hell so that the rest of us can stay here." I lifted my hand to where he clutched my face. My fingers laced with his, so that our bodies were locked together like matching puzzle pieces. "We fought him before in a different life. Let's do it again."

A low growl rumbled in his throat. "And we lost. He destroyed you and wiped my memories. He could very well do the same thing again."

"And I'll find my way back to you if he does," I said softly. "No matter what he throws at us, he can never rip us apart. Not permanently. And he knows it."

"Well if you're going, we're going." Serena and Priyanka popped up beside us with stern looks on their faces. "It's close enough to a full moon, and my wolf is hungry for Lucifer's blood."

I pulled away from Az and gave my best friend a pointed look. "That's creepy, Serena."

She shot me a wolfish smile. "Creepy was exactly what I was going for, so yay."

Priyanka held up a finger. "I'm not sure about the whole blood thing, but I'm a fan of fighting the demon king."

Az grunted and pushed away from us. The four of us folded our arms and watched him pace the full length of the penthouse. When he twisted on his heels, he caught us all staring at him. Shaking his head, he let out a chuckle of annoyance.

"You know, I am the First Prince of Hell." He jerked his thumb toward his chest. "I can order you all to stand down."

"Sure you can." I shrugged. "Doesn't mean we'll listen."

"Maybe I'll lock you up in my bedroom," he shot back.

"All of us?" I arched a brow and turned toward Caim. "Even him?"

Az fisted his hands. "If that's what it takes to keep you safe."

"It's *my* decision, Az."

Asmodeus stared at me across the room, conflicted emotions churning in the depths of his eyes. Shadows glided along his skin like ribbons of silk, and a dark tension pounded through the penthouse like a hammer against steel. I understood that all he wanted was to keep me safe. I couldn't fault him for that. But this was my decision. This whole thing had started because of Az and me. I had to be there when we ended it.

"Fuck," he said with a growl, jamming his fingers into his hair. "Fine. We'll do this together. But if something goes wrong, you have to do everything I say. No heroics, Mia. Got it?"

I smiled. "We'll face down the King of Hell together."

28

Normally, on a night like tonight, *Infernal's* walls would be thumping from the bass. A packed dance floor would be lit up by the strobing golden lights. The dancers would be in their elevated birdcages, swaying to the beat. And Az would roam the floor to meet his most distinguished guests.

Movie stars, singers, internet personalities.

Infernal was famous among the supernatural elite.

Not tonight. The club was dark. The doors were locked tight. It felt like a ghost town.

Or a tomb.

Az unlocked the back door and motioned the team inside. I had a little bounce in my step, fuelled by the nerves sizzling through my veins. This was kind of scary, but I'd be lying if I didn't admit it was also kind of exciting. *Finally*, I was doing something useful. I'd spent a lot of time running and even more time hiding. I was ready to face the music, even if it was a chorus of demons as they dragged me into Hell.

Obviously, I hoped for the total opposite of that. We'd defeat Lucifer, and then everyone would live happily ever after. Of course, life wasn't like a fairy tale. There was still the small matter of Lucifer's throne. It would go to Az. But we'd tackle that complication when we came to it.

"Where will he be?" I whispered, mincing down the corridor on the tiptoes of my heavy black boots. We were on a secret mission. If we made one wrong move, we'd alert the enemy of our arrival. Like Tom Cruise in *Mission Impossible*.

Maybe we should have come in through the air ducts.

Az and everyone else just walked normally. Spoil sports.

"In the club's main room," Az said, raising his brows as I continued to whisper across the floor like a phantom wraith. "Why are you walking like that?"

"So he can't hear us coming."

His lips quirked. "He knows we're coming, Mia. I'm pretty sure he watched us walk through the door."

"Right." I started walking normally, but that meant I no longer had anything to distract me from the fact we were walking straight into the most deadly situation I'd certainly ever been in. Once, we'd gone up against two fallen angels, but we'd had a full Legion against them. Then there was that time that Az had pretended to sacrifice me. At the time, I hadn't understood what was happening, and I'd been pretty terrified. But my life had never really been in jeopardy then. Okay, maybe just a little.

This was the King of Hell. The demon who had already killed me once in another life. Just because it hadn't been *this* body didn't make the memories any less real. I could still feel the terror of that moment. It haunted me in my dreams.

"You ready?" Az slowed to a stop outside the stage door that led into the main section of the club. I knew if I told him I'd changed my mind, he'd walk through that door right now and give himself up to Lucifer. No questions asked.

Which was why I nodded and squeezed his hand.

Together, the five of us pushed out onto the dance floor. Lucifer stood in the center of the quiet space, flipping through a book with a symbol on the front. A pentagram.

He lifted his eyes from the pages and snapped the book shut with a smile. "Ah. Interesting little collection of supernaturals you've brought with you. Two demons, a fae, a wolf, and a human all walked into a bar. There's a joke in there somewhere."

"I'm here to make the trade," Az growled.

Short and to the point, like always.

"Of course you are." Lucifer's gaze shifted to my face, and he scowled. "What's *this* all about, then? Why's your hair brown?"

"I wanted a change." I gave him a blinding smile. "After you complimented the red, I suddenly hated it. Funny that."

We'd decided to leave my hair alone. At least until this was over. It helped solidify our story. Az had decided to go with Lucifer because I'd disguised myself and run off. Kind of like what actually had happened. Only in our fake version, he'd decided to leave earth so I could stay.

It was close enough to the truth that Lucifer might actually buy it.

Fingers crossed.

"No, you're hiding something." Lucifer waggled his finger and sniffed the air. "You changed your scent, too." His eyes slightly widened. "You were trying to hide from *him*."

My mouth dropped open as I faked surprise. "But how did you...?"

Lucifer laughed. "You're far too easy to read, Mia. That's why you never stood a chance against me. You're like an open book. I've seen all your moves coming a mile away."

I bit back the urge to say something snarky. Az stepped up to my side, placing a firm hand on my shoulder. "Which is why I'm not going to let her give up her life when there's a better option. I've decided to go back to Hell with you."

Lucifer's smile stretched wide. "Good. You've finally come to your senses. It's where you belong, Asmodeus. Not here with all these mortals and weak supernaturals like fae and wolves. Hell is your home."

"It is my home. However..." Az released his grip on my shoulder and edged in front of me. "You made an offer. The demons in my Legion are to go free, as well as Mia."

Lucifer's smile vanished, and his gaze went hard. "Hell is the Legion's home, too, Asmodeus. One might wonder why they'd wish to stay here in a world full of mortals."

Az folded his arms and stared down his King. "You made an offer. If they wish to stay here, it's their decision to make. If you back out of this now, I walk away."

An animalistic growl rumbled in Lucifer's throat, and his eyes sharpened like twin knives. Anger rippled off him, and I swore I could feel the heat of it slam against my skin.

His eyes cut my way, and for a moment, I felt like I could read his thoughts. Lucifer had hoped Az would never give in to his demands. He wanted to see me suffer. He wanted to rip me apart and watch me burn.

So why hadn't he killed me? Was it because it hadn't worked the first time? If he tried again, I'd only come back. Next time, he might not be able to find me.

What he wanted most was to keep me away from Az.

But why? It made no sense. Sure, he was the King of Hell, and I knew I could never fully understand the motivations for what he did. He was in the midst of a celestial game for souls, and humans were nothing but pawns to him. How could I ever understand the actions of someone like that?

There still had to be an explanation. One he kept close to his chest.

"Fine." Lucifer relaxed, shuttering his vicious anger. "I will stick to my end of the bargain if it means you will never have contact with Mia McNally again. You must remain in Hell until she is gone from this world."

Az's hands fisted. "Agreed. Now where is my Legion?"

Lucifer laughed. "Oh, Asmodeus. Sometimes I forget how single-minded you can get. Your Legion has been here the entire time."

I straightened, my gaze darting around the silent club. There was no sign of the Legion anywhere. They couldn't be here unless...

Dropping back my head, I stared up at the elevated birdcages. Four of the six held prisoners, each with a sock in his mouth. Phenex, Valac, Bael, and Stolas. They were all there. And based on the flashes of anger in their eyes, they were fine. Just a little pissed off.

Okay, a *lot* pissed off.

And they'd been here the whole time. At any point, we could have easily found them. Lucifer had put them right under our noses, and we hadn't even thought to check. Unfortunately, I couldn't get to them. The ladder leading up to the ceiling was gone. I kind of wanted to punch the demon king to make a point, but I didn't think that would go over very well.

I'd get my chance to hit him where it hurt soon enough. Just had to play Little Miss Nice Human a bit longer. As soon as Caim gave me the signal, I'd blast Lucifer with the ring.

"Caim," Az barked. "Get them down from there."

"No," Lucifer said, his voice full of steel. "You will come with me through the gate, and *then* Caim can release them."

Even though Lucifer had said the very thing we'd feared the most, my ears pricked up a little. The gate? What was that all about? My memories of my previous life as a fallen angel didn't extend past anything that didn't involve Az. So I still didn't understand how all this worked. I knew demons and fallen angels could travel to the underworld, but I didn't know how.

"Where's the gate?" I couldn't help but ask.

Lucifer gave me a strange look. "Where's the gate? You don't remember?"

"Should I? I'm not a demon and never have been."

"How odd." He cocked his head. "And here I assumed all of your memories had returned to you."

I glanced at Az. "The important ones did."

"The gate is below *Infernal*," Az said quietly with a glance over his shoulder. His eyes met mine, but in his attempt to close himself off to Lucifer, I couldn't read him, either. "It's underground."

Of course it was. The gate to Hell couldn't be somewhere cheery, like the middle of Central Park or something. No doubt there were dog-sized rats down there, waiting to nibble on someone's toes. It would be dark and dreary. The kind of place the clown from *It* would hang out.

So obviously that was where we'd have to go.

"After you," Lucifer motioned toward Az.

When I made a move to follow, the King of Hell stepped in my path. "Where do you think you're going?"

"Um. Down into the creepy hellgate dungeon."

He flashed me his teeth, and it sent a shudder down my spine. "You aren't going through the gate. You're to stay here. That's the entire point of this deal."

Heart hammering, I glanced over my shoulder at Caim. His face was impossible to read, just like

Az's. They'd clearly had a lot of practice at stuff like this, but how was I supposed to know what to do now? This wasn't part of the plan. We needed to stick together if we wanted to have any chance of beating Lucifer.

"Aren't you at least going to let me say goodbye to him?" I finally asked. "It's bad enough you're taking him away from me forever."

Lucifer sneered. "I could make things easier on you, if you'd like. I've erased your memories once. I can do it again."

I stiffened and took a big step back. "No, please don't do that."

"Then you'll stay *here*," he said in a venomous growl before lifting his eyes to the demon who stood behind me. "Caim, you come. I won't have you flying up to release the Legion until after Az has walked through that gate."

"Sure," Caim said with a shrug.

Lucifer turned his sharp gaze on Serena and Priyanka, who'd nervously stayed silent during the entire exchange. "The wolf and the fae stay here, too."

With that, the demons strode purposefully out the door, leaving me and the girls alone beneath the elevated cages. This wasn't good. While Caim and Az were strong, the entire plan revolved around catching Lucifer off guard. He no doubt suspected we were up to something. Otherwise, he wouldn't have been so insistent to split us up.

"What do we do now?" Pri whispered, stepping up to my side to stare after the retreating demons.

"Cause utter chaos?" I tried.

Serena stepped up to my other side. "And how are we going to do that?"

I dropped back my head to stare up at the cages. The demons had started to get a tad agitated over the past few moments when they'd realized what Az planned to do. The cages were squealing, rocking angrily on the metal chains.

"Release the Legion. Lucifer will never know what's hit him."

29

"Sounds like a great idea, Mia," Priyanka said. "But, um, the ladder's gone."

I held up Az's ring. "I'm going to blast this at the ground so it will shoot me up to the ceiling."

Serena and Priyanka stared at me with matching blank expressions. They seemed almost dumfounded by my words, and I couldn't really blame them. In my head, it had made a lot more sense. I'd aim the ring's power at the floor, and the force would shoot me up to the demons.

Hey, that kind of thing worked in the movies, right?

"Az would absolutely kill me if I let you do that," Priyanka said flatly. "You're more likely to break your neck than reach the cages. How the hell would you get down?"

"They have wings." I shrugged. "I'd let one of

them out, and they can take care of everything else."

Serena narrowed her eyes. "For a second there, I thought this was a bad joke, but now I'm seeing you're actually serious about this."

"Do you have a better idea?" I asked.

"Yes," she said. "Knock you out so you can't do anything stupid."

I gave her a wry smile. "Perfect. That will definitely stop Lucifer from dragging Az back to Hell."

"Eh, maybe we should let her try it," Pri said with a shrug. "We can be ready to catch her in case it goes wrong."

Serena moved toward Priyanka like a lioness. "Have both of you lost your goddamn minds? I don't care what happened in some past life, Mia is a human now and—"

While they were busy bickering, I decided to take matters into my own hands. I wrapped my fingers around the ring and focused. In the past, the power had just come to me when I needed it the most. So I had to convey the seriousness of the situation to the ring.

Please, I whispered to it. *You're Az's ring. Can't you sense he needs your help? Get me up to the ceiling so I can let the others out.*

The ring buzzed to life. Flames of power raced up my arm and buried themselves in my heart. Pain thundered through me with the intensity of the magic, too much for my human body to hold. It exploded out of me and slammed into the ground. With a shriek, I launched up toward the cages.

My arms and legs flailed as I was momentarily suspended in the air. Fear throttled my heart; my breath stuck in my throat. I glanced down at the floor. Pri and Serena stared up at me, jaws dropped. My god, the floor was far away.

Time to shove away that fear. Swallowing hard, I turned my attention up. The nearest cage, holding Phenex, was almost in my grasp. With eager fingers, I reached out. My fingers skimmed the metal bars. And then gravity took control.

I started to fall.

Panic ripped through me. With a scream, I grabbed at the cage, desperately trying to catch myself before I plummeted to the ground. I'd already used one blast. It would take time for the ring to charge back up again. I couldn't screw this up. It might be our only chance to give Az the backup he needed to face down his King.

Plus, I really didn't want to break all the bones in my body when I hit the floor.

A strange lightness filled my veins. It happened in the blink of an eye, too fast for me to truly understand it. And then I reached out, grabbed the bars, and pulled myself up to where Lucifer had left the key jammed into the lock.

Huh. That was weird.

Phenex stared out at me with wide, eager eyes. He shouted against his sock, but I couldn't make out his words. With a deep breath, I twisted the lock and pulled.

The door swung wide and took me with it. I screamed, clutching the bars as my legs flailed beneath me. The cage shuddered and shook, almost knocking me off. I squeezed my eyes tight and tried to count to ten. I needed to calm my terror, but my hands had become slick with sweat. I wasn't going to be able to hold on for much longer.

Suddenly, a strong pair of hands wrapped around me and gently pulled me away from the cage. Phenex gathered me into his arms and soared down to the floor, where Serena and Priyanka were pacing back and forth. His wings thundered behind him as he set me down, and then he was off, unlocking the rest of the cages.

The reunion was short and to the point. The Legion surrounded me, thundering me on the back and roaring my name. Their frantic energy turned toward the door, and then they stormed out of the main room to follow the others. It was a whirlwind of insanity. By the time they were gone, it was all I could do to breathe.

I smiled. *Good luck, Lucifer.*

Checkmate.

"What are we still doing here?" Priyanka asked when the silence descended upon us. "Come on. Don't you want to see this?"

"Yeah." I laughed. "I definitely do."

We took off after the Legion, following the

sound of thundering footsteps. It took us to a hidden set of stairs that wound down into the dark. I winced and exchanged uneasy glances with the girls, but it wasn't like the shadows would stop us now.

Racing down the stairs, we stumbled into a room that could only be described as a dungeon. Instruments of torture lined the stone walls. Stakes and chains. Metal contraptions and spiky wheels. Flickering torches lit up the dark space, highlighting a path that led further into the darkness.

"Maybe this wasn't such a good idea," Serena said, her voice echoing against the stone walls.

I bit my lips. This was weird. Now that we were down here, the sound of the demons' footsteps had faded into nothing more than the *drip, drip, drip* of nearby water.

Where had they gone? Where was the damn gate? Had I taken too long to release the Legion?

Had they all gone to Hell?

"Well, this has taken a dramatically creepy turn," I muttered, taking a step away from the tunnel of darkness. "Can you still hear them?"

Serena let out a low whistle and shook her head. "No. That's the strangest thing about this. As soon as we stepped out of that stairwell, the footsteps stopped. It's like they came this way, but then..."

I swallowed hard and stared into the darkness.

Vanished.

Surely not. There would have been a fight.

Lucifer might be the King of Hell, but there was only one of him. He couldn't just snap his fingers and smite six fully formed adult Princes of Hell. Could he?

"So where's this gate?" I turned to ask Priyanka, but she was no longer by my side. Frowning, I whirled on my feet, only to find that Serena wasn't with me anymore, either. Dread coiled like a snake, ready to strike its venom into my heart. Blood roaring in my ears, I slowly stepped back toward the stairwell, scarcely daring to make a single sound.

Something weird was going on here.

"Serena?" I whisper-called to the dungeon. "Priyanka?"

I didn't want to shout too loud. One of the lessons I'd learned from watching lots of horror movies was to never, ever wander around a creepy dungeon shouting for your missing friends. That was a great way to catch the killer's attention.

No one answered my call.

Right. Time to listen to logic. People didn't just *vanish*. There was something else going on here. A fae glamor of some sort. The others had run up against it, and it was hiding them. Or something like that. Serena would never leave me alone down here, so I knew she hadn't raced up the stairs to safety. I doubted Priyanka would have, either. She was a good egg.

They had to be down here somewhere. I just

couldn't see them.

With a deep breath, I paced from one end of the dungeon to the next. I needed some help, and who better to assist with a fae glamor than the fae themselves? I grabbed my phone and punched in the number, only to realize there was no service underground.

Pressing my lips together, I cast a quick glance behind me and headed to the stairwell. I only needed a minute to make the call, and then I'd come back down here to wait on the fae, just in case something happened.

I raced up the winding stairs. My footsteps were loud against my ears, a sudden contrast to the eerie silence of the dungeon. When I reached the top landing, I shoved the door. It didn't budge.

Frowning, I shoved harder.

It didn't even crack an inch.

Adrenaline pumping through my veins, I threw all my weight behind my shoulder and slammed against the wood. Pain flared through my left arm, sharp and electric. I stumbled back and stared.

My lungs stilled. With timid fingers, I twisted the knob one more time and pushed. The door would not open. I'd been locked in. No one else was with me. My heart thundered against my ribs. *He'd* done this. It was the only explanation.

I'd somehow stumbled right into another one of Lucifer's traps.

He had me right where he wanted me.

30

Okay. No need to panic. So what if the King of Hell had sneakily trapped me inside a dungeon packed full of medieval torture devices? It could definitely be worse. For example, there could be horned creatures crawling around down here trying to eat me, and so far I hadn't seen any sign of that.

Knock on wood.

So what now? As far as I could tell, I had two options. I could keep banging on this door and hoping I could break it down by sheer force of will. My hands might shatter in the process, and there would probably be some blood. Or I could search the dungeon for another exit.

I wasn't particularly fond of either of these options. The dungeon was...weird. People kept vanishing. I didn't know if it had something to do with the gate to Hell, and I really didn't want to

291

find out. But banging on the door wasn't going to get me anywhere. Not unless someone showed up at the club to check things out. Everyone who might fall into that category had walked down these stairs.

To the dungeon it was.

After tiptoeing back down the stairs, I eyeballed the torch-lit path that led to who knew where. It was the only way out of this main room. Before I made my move, I wandered over to the wall and grabbed one of the spikey things. Heavy and metallic, it looked like it could pound through steel.

Let's see how Lucifer enjoys having this pointed at his face.

I took the path out of the main room. It tunnelled through rock, twisting and turning so quickly that it was impossible to see more than a few steps ahead. That, plus the darkness, made me feel as though I was so far beneath the earth that it would take me hours to reach the surface.

The further I walked, the more time I had to think. I didn't understand what had happened, but something had gone terribly wrong. Az and the other demons had vanished. So had the girls. It didn't seem like a coincidence or a random accident. Nothing ever was when Lucifer was involved.

He'd planned this. He'd known that we weren't going to go along with his deal, no matter what we told him. He'd put assurances into place, designed to stop us from working against him.

Despair pressed down on me, as heavy as lead.

With every step I took, it only got heavier. We'd all made a terrible mistake. We should have done something more random, something harder for him to anticipate. Lucifer had moved his little pieces around the board and watched as we slid ours exactly where he'd expected.

If I could go back in time and change it, I would.

I finally reached the end of the path. From here, it branched in opposite directions. One path led into darkness, the other toward light. I shifted on my feet. Lucifer would expect me to choose the lit path.

Gritting my teeth, I turned toward the shadows and followed the darkness down into the earth. Time ticked by slowly. My steps were quiet and short. I didn't dare walk too quickly for fear I'd stumble upon a sudden cliff and tumble to my death.

The path opened up into an enormous cavern. A glimmering seal shimmered in the distance. Flames whorled around the symbol, sparking up the cavern with orange light. I ducked behind a boulder and stared, heart thundering in my chest. I recognized that seal. It was Lucifer's.

Twice as tall as I was, the glowing seal hummed with a powerful energy that set my teeth on edge. My mouth went dry. I had a sneaking suspicion I knew exactly what that thing was. A gate. A portal. A first-class ticket to Hell.

Voices echoed off the walls. With my breath in my throat, I ducked behind the boulder and shoved my back against the rough stone. Two pairs of footsteps headed my way. I tried to calm my breathing. Demons had enhanced hearing. Any sound I made would snag their attention in an instant.

A familiar voice filled the cavern. "Thank you for your help tonight, Rafael. Everything is finally going according to plan."

Chills swept down my arms. Rafael. *Noah.* Lucifer had brought him here to help with the standoff against Az. He hadn't been alone when the Legion had stormed into the dungeon. It might have been enough to even out the fight.

Shit. Heart pounding, I loosed a silent breath and pulled another in.

"My pleasure," Rafael replied. "Asmodeus has gone far too long without facing repercussions for his actions. I've been trying to tell you for years. I'm glad you finally saw the light."

"Careful," Lucifer said, his tone lethal. "I do not appreciate being questioned by the likes of you. There is no loyalty between us, Rafael. Wrong me, and I would not hesitate to make your fate the same as theirs."

A knife of pain stabbed my heart. Hands fisting, I bit my lip to stop myself from crying. *The same fate.* Surely that couldn't mean what it sounded like. *Death.* It wasn't possible. Az was the strongest person I'd ever met. He couldn't have gone down that easily. And yet...where was he? Where were the others? Lucifer had done something, but what?

Rafael cleared his throat uneasily. "Of course, Your Highness."

"Good." Lucifer's voice echoed as he drifted through the room. "You're learning quickly."

Rafael followed him toward the gate. Their voices were growing distant, and most of their words were hard to make out from this far away. With a deep breath, I darted from one boulder to the next. I needed to hear what he said. Maybe Az was still alive, trapped somewhere.

"So what's next?" Rafael asked. "Where do we go from here?"

I could hear the danger in Lucifer's voice far before I felt it. "Mia McNally is here in the dungeon. It's time to hunt her down."

31

That was all I needed to hear. I crouch-walked away from the boulder, darted toward the next rock, and then practically crawled the rest of the way out of the hellgate room. When I made it to safety—*ha!*—I let out a long, shuddering breath. Lucifer was still by the gate with Rafael, and I could no longer make out their words. Maybe they couldn't hear me, either.

Right. I couldn't focus on Az and the others right now. If I did, it might crush me. Lucifer hadn't said he'd actually killed them, so there was still a chance they were alive.

There was another option. He'd sent them to Hell. I didn't know how he'd gotten them from A to B without so much as a shout, but that was what I was working with right now.

As I crept down the tunnel away from Lucifer, there was a part of me that wanted to rush straight

toward him and beg to be taken into the underworld. I wanted to reach Az. I wanted to get Serena
and Priyanka out of there. I couldn't stand the
thought of any of them trapped in that horrible
place forever.

There had to be something I could do.

But I couldn't be certain that was even where
they were. And right now, Lucifer was hunting me.

When I reached the fork in the path, I took the
tunnel toward the light.

I needed to remember that I was the only one
left. If I let myself get caught, I'd be no help to
anyone. Besides, I'd never been to Hell before. What
was it like? Was it just a bunch of volcanoes and fire
pits? Were there cities? How did I avoid getting
eaten by monsters?

All very valid questions, and I had zero answers.
Az had never wanted to talk about it, and I couldn't
blame him. If Lucifer loved the place, it probably
sucked.

At the end of the tunnel, I reached another
cavernous room. Street lamps shone through the
sidewalk grates high above, casting light upon a
maze of stalagmites. Their sharp points rose from
the ground like a bizarre collection of vampire teeth.

My hope deflated. I'd chosen this route,
thinking I'd find something other than rocks and
emptiness. Although...there *was* a way out in this
room. Maybe they'd all gotten away. I tipped back
my head and gazed up at the grates. With wings,

they'd be able to force their way back into Manhattan.

And if Serena and Priyanka had been with them, the demons could have taken them out of here, too.

The only problem with my little theory was the fact that none of them would have left me alone in here with Lucifer.

"Mia!" Lucifer's voice rang out behind me, echoing off the cavernous walls.

My heart rattled. I dove into the maze of stalagmites, scrabbling out of sight. His footsteps were the only sound that followed as he strode into the room. Fear pounded in my veins. Surely he could smell that.

"It's pointless to hide, Mia," he said. "You're in here all alone, and you have no one left to protect you."

I glanced down at the metal stake in my hand. There was no one around to protect me, but at least I had this. I wondered if he'd considered that when moving his little chess pieces around the board. Did he know I'd be more than willing to ram this thing into his heart?

Come at me, I thought, tightening my grip around the steel. He thought of me as a helpless human. And you know what? That was fine. The more he underestimated me, the more satisfying it would be when I beat him at his own game.

He'd won far too many times. He'd taken my past life. And now, he'd taken Az from me. I might not be the strongest fighter out there, but I'd never give up.

It's not about how hard you hit. It's about how hard you *get hit*, and then stand up again for more. *Thanks, Rocky.*

Lucifer let out a frustrated sigh as he wandered through the cave. "This is very tiresome. You do know you have no hope of an escape."

He rounded one of the stalagmites close to me. Gritting my teeth, I scuttled to the side, ducking behind a larger rock just before he spotted me.

Lucifer froze. So did I. There was no doubt in my mind he'd probably heard me, but that didn't mean he could pinpoint my exact location.

"Do you know what lions like to do with their prey, Mia?" he asked from where he still stood, only a few inches away from where I hid.

Obviously I didn't answer. Did he really think I was that dumb?

"They stalk them," he hissed. "They sometimes like to play with their food. It's a great game at times, but eventually, they grow bored with it."

Mouth dry, I poked my head around the stalagmite and gazed at the tunnel that would lead me out of here. The problem was, I had nowhere to go. If I went back to the stairwell, the bolted door would block my exit. If I returned to the other cavern, the only way out was Hell.

And Lucifer knew it.

No matter how well I hid. No matter how long I

evaded capture...none of it mattered. Because I couldn't go anywhere. I didn't have wings to take me to the safety of the sidewalk, and I didn't have the brute force to knock down doors.

I fingered the ring around my neck. This was the only power I had, and I'd already used it up. It had never come back to me so quickly after a blast.

But it's all I've got.

He sighed again. "You do know I can smell you, right?"

Slowly, I pushed up from the ground on wobbly legs. Lucifer stood just before me, a wicked smile curling his full lips. His eyes flicked toward the stake in my hands. Good. The perfect distraction.

My other palm squeezed the ring as my mind called upon Az's power. Magic blasted from deep within my gut and hurtled toward the King. It hit him square in the chest. Eyes wide, he stumbled back.

And then I ran.

32

I'd never run faster in my life. Arms pumping, heart racing, I soared down the tunnel with an invisible wind at my back. Adrenaline surged through my veins, giving me a boost I sorely needed.

I'd used Az's power against Lucifer.

It had worked!

When I reached the fork in the tunnel, I swung a right. My boots pounded the ground like thunder. I stumbled into the torture room and spun onward to the stairs. I had no idea how I'd gotten Az's ring to work a second time so quickly, but I wasn't done with it yet. By sheer force of will, I was going to make that damn ring listen to me.

I threw myself up the stairs. Fingers clutching the ring, I squeezed my eyes and focused with all the strength and determination in my soul. Power rumbled beneath my skin—slower than last time but still very much there. It bubbled through my pores and shot toward the door and—

A hand gripped my arm. It pulled me back. The ground vanished from beneath my feet, and darkness consumed me.

I think I screamed, but it was impossible to tell. The darkness was absolute, like an infinity of nothingness. Sorrow filled my soul as I tried to make sense of it. It was like the world no longer existed anymore. *I* no longer existed.

And then everything shuddered back into place.

My feet hit the ground. The darkness poofed away. Sights and sounds roared around me, filling my head with static. I blinked, vision clearing. I was standing in the goddamn hellgate room.

Rafael stepped away from me and brushed his hands against his jeans. I shot him a glare. "You used your weird shadowy magic to teleport me. Didn't you?"

"If you hadn't tried to escape, it wouldn't have been necessary."

All I could do was stare at him. It still unnerved me, seeing him like this. Once, I'd thought he was a boring, slightly insufferable hipster who loved coffee and my best friend. Now he was the dick who'd tried to kill me. More than once. And he'd murdered dozens of other supernaturals.

"What did you do with Serena?" I asked through gritted teeth.

"Serena is fine. We didn't want any werewolves

making things more complicated. You should thank me. Normally I would have just killed her." He shrugged. "I took her and the fae to her apartment in Brooklyn. By the time she gets here again, we'll all be long gone."

The hellgate shimmered before us, casting eerie orange light upon the stone walls. "Because you're taking me to Hell."

"That's the idea."

"But why?"

"You'll have to ask him." Rafael turned toward the tunnel entrance as Lucifer approached. He strolled toward us with his hands slung into his pockets and a slightly annoyed expression on his face.

Looked like I hadn't done any permanent damage. That was a shame.

"Nice try, Mia," Lucifer said easily as he joined us by the gate. "I didn't expect you to be so bold. I won't make the same mistake again."

I bent my knees and sliced the stake toward him.

He stepped back, arching a brow. "Lars was right about your feistiness. Do you have any idea who it is you're trying to fight?"

"Yes," I hissed, feeling a bit feral. "The King of Hell."

"And what exactly do you think you're going to do with that?"

"I mean, the first thought that pops into my mind is that I want to shove it right into your face.

305

But I figure the heart is better. Or maybe your neck. That way I can separate your head from your body and bury you thousands of miles apart."

"I see Az has been sharing our secrets," Lucifer said with an ease that made my head spin. The least he could do was look a little bit nervous.

"It sounds like you're not willing to fight me." I shot him a smile that matched his own. "Are you scared of the angry human?"

He rolled his eyes. "Please. Your little act is tiresome. I know you don't really want to fight me."

"Actually, I do." I inched a little closer, wafting my scent toward him. "Take a sniff and tell me I'm not dying for a fight."

Lucifer's lips flatlined. He huffed out a sigh of annoyance, but I knew I had him hooked. With pinned eyes, he sniffed, and then his gaze sharpened on my face. "Interesting. Most humans would run screaming in the other direction when faced with the hellgate."

"I'm not really a human," I said. "And nothing you can do will ever make me run screaming."

His smile widened. "I'm afraid I'm going to have to prove you wrong, Mia McNally." He held out his hand toward Rafael. "My sword."

My heart stopped. "Wait a minute. No swords."

"You have a weapon." He nodded at the stake. "It's only fair if I have one as well."

Shit. I took a step back.

Rafael reached behind him and pulled a sword

out of thin air. He passed it to Lucifer, grinning. I wet my lips and tried not to panic when he slid the weapon from its scabbard. It was massive. At least as tall as me and almost as wide. I'd never seen anything like it before, and I was pretty sure it could chop down an entire tree in one blow.

It had to weigh at least a hundred pounds.

He wouldn't even have to stab me with it. One tap on the head, and I'd be out.

Squaring my shoulders, I lifted my stake—that now looked tiny—before me. Lucifer spun the sword in his hands, whistling an eerie tune that sounded horrifyingly familiar. It sounded like death and pain and fear. The melody dug into my skin and stayed there.

I shook my head to block it out. He was trying to unnerve me, and it was working. And I didn't want to give him the satisfaction.

The bastard.

He flipped his sword. I angled my stake. And then he swung. Everything happened in the blink of an eye. The sword arced through the air, hurtling right toward my throat. A scream ripped from the very depths of me as my life flashed before my eyes.

Az and me. Then and now.

The memories filled my mind until it was all I could see.

With a roar, Lucifer swung the blade up toward the ceiling just a second before it would have sliced my head clean off my body. The sword tumbled out of his hands and clattered across the stone floor. It slid through the hellgate and vanished from the cave.

I gaped at him, my chest heaving.

I'd been two seconds away from death, and then—

He'd saved me?

"What was that?" I whispered. "Why did you stop yourself?"

Lucifer's face hardened. "You're mistaken."

"No." I shook my head and stepped toward him. "That sword was about to go right through my neck. *You stopped it.*"

Lucifer growled, fisting his hands. Rafael had slowly started inching away, almost as though he feared what would happen next. The King of Hell had clearly spared me. But why? None of this made any sense. He'd killed me in a past life, and he'd had it out for me ever since.

There was something I was missing. Memories were still lost to me. Lucifer wanted to keep me away from Az, but he wasn't willing to kill me. He needed me for something else.

And I refused to give him the chance.

With a low growl, I lunged toward him with my stake raised. His lips parted. I slammed the weapon into his chest. It sliced through his clothes and burrowed into his chest. Blood poured from the wound, painting my hands.

Swallowing hard, I released my grip.

His hands latched around mine, holding me there. His eyes lit with fire. "You shouldn't have done that."

"You've given me no other choice," I spat into his face. "This has to end. Here and now. I'm no longer going to play your stupid games. I'm done being your pawn, your plaything. This is *my* life, the only one I have left after you took the last one from me. And I'm going to live it the way I want."

Tears poured down my face. I hadn't realized how much pain and anger had built inside of me. It was desperate to get out.

Lucifer tipped back his head and laughed. His hands still latched around mine, he yanked the stake out of his chest and shoved me back. Heart pounding, I stumbled away as his skin shuddered back into place, as smooth and unmarked as if I'd never stabbed him.

"I am the King of Hell." He stalked toward me. "You cannot harm me, Mia McNally."

I spun on my heels to run, but his hands latched onto my arms before I could even make it a single step. He threw me over his shoulder like I weighed nothing at all and darted through the cavern at a speed that could rival the sun.

He dropped me on the floor beside the gate. Tears burning my eyes, I tried to crawl away, but he grabbed my feet and tugged me back.

My scream was the last thing I heard as he dragged me into Hell.

ACKNOWLEDGMENTS

As always, I want to thank my husband for the support and encouragement during writing this book. I couldn't do it without you!

A big thank you goes to my online writing friends: Christine, Frankie, Alison, Tammi, Jen, and Marina. And everyone in the AC. Your daily chats help keep me going.

And, of course, to my readers. I'm so thrilled that you've enjoyed this series so far. Thank you for all of your support!

ALSO BY JENNA WOLFHART

The Mist King

Of Mist and Shadow

Of Ash and Embers

Of Night and Chaos

The Fallen Fae

Court of Ruins

Kingdom in Exile

Keeper of Storms

Tower of Thorns

Realm of Ashes

Prince of Shadows (A Novella)

Demons After Dark: Covenant

Devilish Deal

Infernal Games

Wicked Oath

Demons After Dark: Temptation

Sinful Touch

Darkest Fate

Hellish Night